Millie's Remarkable Journey

BOOK THREE
of the
A Life of Faith:
Millie Keith
Series

Based on the beloved books by
Martha Finley

MCP
Mission City Press
Franklin, Tennessee

Book Three of the *A Life of Faith: Millie Keith* Series

Millie's Remarkable Journey
Copyright © 2002, Mission City Press, Inc. All Rights Reserved.

Published by Mission City Press, Inc.

This book is based on the *Mildred Keith* novels written by Martha Finley and first published in 1876 by Dodd, Mead & Company.

Adaptation Written by:	Kersten Hamilton
Cover & Interior Design:	Richmond & Williams
Cover Photography:	Michelle Grisco Photography
Typesetting:	BookSetters

For more information, write to Mission City Press at 202 Second Avenue South, Franklin, Tennessee 37064, or visit our Web Site at:

www.alifeoffaith.com

Library of Congress Catalog Card Number: 2001092286
Finley, Martha
    Millie's Remarkable Journey
    Book Three of the *A Life of Faith: Millie Keith* Series
    ISBN-13: 978-1-928749-11-0
    ISBN-10: 1-928749-11-9

Printed in the United States of America
3 4 5 6 7 8 9 10 — 11 10 09 08 07 06

DEDICATION

This book is
dedicated to
the memory of
MARTHA FINLEY
1828—1909

*Martha Finley was a woman of God
clearly committed to advancing the cause of Christ
through stories of people who sought
to reflect Christian character in everyday life.
Although written in an era very different from ours,
her works still inspire both young and old
to seek to know and follow the living God.*

— FOREWORD —

*I*n this book, the third of the *A Life of Faith: Millie Keith* Series, you are invited to continue learning about the past as you grow in faith with Millie.

Our story resumes in early October of 1836 in the frontier town of Pleasant Plains, Indiana. Millie Keith is now fifteen years old, just two months away from her sixteenth birthday. The previous two years have passed quickly. The town has grown as most towns on the frontier were doing at that time. And although it is nothing like the thriving, established town of Lansdale, Ohio, which the Keiths left behind when they moved to Indiana three years earlier, Pleasant Plains has truly come to feel like home to all the family. Millie and her parents and her seven brothers and sisters have established friendships with the townsfolk, and each member of the Keith family has adjusted in his or her own way to the customs and challenges of their new life. Milking the cow, raising chickens, and constantly shaking sand out of shoes have become a normal part of everyday life.

Unfortunately, the past two years have not been easy for Millie. Greatly weakened from battling the widespread ague that swept through the town in the summer of 1834, Millie has spent the past two winters trying to clear the illness from her lungs. She has done her best to be "strong and of good courage," but her parents are understandably concerned as she has grown paler and thinner. They worry that the upcoming winter might make her worse. Millie's parents long to send her to a milder climate to recover, but cannot afford the cost of such a journey. Yet their hope in God is firm, and the incredible Keith family faces life and all its challenges head-on, with the Word of God to guide them. God's answer to their plea sets Millie on a long journey where she encounters a different way of life with pre-Civil War challenges.

Millie's Remarkable Journey is an adaptation of the Mildred Keith novels originally published in 1876. In bringing Millie's story to life for today's readers, many changes have been made. The language has been updated, the plot expanded and enhanced, the characters more fully developed, and the Christian message has been strengthened. In addition, we have added fascinating information on the history and social customs of the time period. This background helps bring the reader into Millie's world and further illuminates her strong Christian character.

∞ **Slavery in Millie's Day** ∞

In 1839 there were 2,700,000 men, women, and children held as slaves in the southern states. Modern books and movies often give the impression that everyone in the South was a slave owner, but that is far from true. The census of 1850 shows that fewer than a third of the six million white people of the South were members of slave-owning families. Of those families who did own slaves, the majority owned fewer than five. Only 254 families owned more than two hundred slaves, and of those, only eleven owned more than five hundred. These powerful, wealthy families were the equivalent of a royal aristocracy, running the governments of their states and moving public sentiment. Small farmers who owned two or three slaves were likely to work alongside them, and much more likely to treat their slaves well.

Millie's Remarkable Journey

Slavery on a Plantation

Most slaves on a plantation were field hands. Men, women, and children over the age of ten worked in the fields. On a typical plantation, their day started very early in the morning (sometimes as early as 4 A.M.) with the blast of a horn that summoned the slaves to work. They scrambled to the fields or threshing halls or wherever they would be working that day. Usually, anyone who was late would be punished — often whipped.

Overseers, generally with whips and pistols or rifles, kept watch over slaves to see that they worked as hard as they could. They used the whips to create fear and to keep the slaves, who outnumbered them, under control.

Most overseers expected men and women to perform the same heavy labor. Women who had recently given birth were typically allowed four weeks to recover before they had to be back in the fields; then they carried their babies with them, and laid them on the ground under a tree or bush while they worked. Sometimes older children of four to six years old watched the babies. Children younger than ten were left in the children's house, under the care of an old woman.

At midday the horn sounded again, and the slaves hurried to their huts, made a fire, and cooked hominy or corn cakes. In many places, this was the only meal of the day. Slaves soon learned to be frugal with their portions. A typical ration was one peck (two dry gallons) of corn per person per week. If corn was not available, the master would provide a peck of potatoes or rice. Not surprisingly, most slaves suffered from exhaustion and malnutrition.

As soon as their food was swallowed, they went back to the fields and worked until their task was done, or until it

was too dark to see. If they did not finish before it was too dark they might be whipped. The horn sounded again at dark, signaling that every slave should be in his or her quarters. Anyone found outside after that could be beaten.

Slaves lived in one-room houses or cabins. Several people, not always related, would share a one-room shack, usually sleeping on the floor. There were seldom beds, chairs, or tables in a slave cabin. There were no stoves and no chimneys. Some huts had crude fireplaces; in others the fire was built in the middle of the floor. They slept in the only clothes they had, which saved time in the morning when they had to run to work.

There were no laws to protect slaves from being whipped, kicked, beaten, starved, branded, chained in irons, or from any other type of torture, and these forms of cruelty were practiced on many large plantations. A master could beat a slave to death with no penalty under the law.

Christianity on the Plantation

Before 1844, many plantation owners would not allow their slaves to hear the Christian Gospel preached. They believed the slaves would begin to think of themselves as the children of Israel in Egypt, oppressed by hard taskmasters. However, Christianity did take hold, even on plantations where the masters tried to keep it out. Slaves would sneak away to secret church meetings after dark. Some paid the ultimate price for their faith in Jesus. In 1839 Sarah Grimke, one of the first women to publicly argue for the abolition of slavery, wrote the following:

"A beloved friend in South Carolina, the wife of a slaveholder, with whom I often mingled my tears, when helpless and hopeless we deplored together the horrors

of slavery, related to me some years since the following circumstance.

"On the plantation adjoining her husband's, there was a slave of pre-eminent piety. His master was not a professor of religion, but the superior excellence of this disciple of Christ was not unmarked by him, and I believe he was so sensible of the good influence of his piety that he did not deprive him of the few religious privileges within his reach. A planter was one day dining with the owner of this slave, and in the course of conversation observed that all profession of religion among slaves was mere hypocrisy. The other asserted a contrary opinion, adding, 'I have a slave who I believe would rather die than deny his Savior.' This was ridiculed, and the master urged to prove the assertion. He accordingly sent for this man of God, and peremptorily ordered him to deny his belief in the Lord Jesus Christ. The slave pleaded to be excused, constantly affirming that he would rather die than deny the Redeemer, whose blood was shed for him. His master, after vainly trying to induce obedience by threats, had him terribly whipped. The fortitude of the sufferer was not to be shaken; he nobly rejected the offer of exemption from further chastisement at the expense of destroying his soul, and this blessed martyr died in consequence of this severe infliction. Oh, how bright a gem will this victim of irresponsible power be, in that crown which sparkles on the Redeemer's brow; and that many such will cluster there, I have not the shadow of a doubt."

Christians prayed, preached, taught the truth, and helped slaves escape in Millie's day. God answered the prayers of His saints. The evil of slavery was eventually broken in the United

States, but not without terrible suffering and great loss of life. On January 1, 1863, after two years of bloody civil war, President Abraham Lincoln issued the Emancipation Proclamation which stated that "all persons held as slaves . . . shall be then, thenceforward, and forever free."

Slavery Today

Unfortunately, the battle against slavery is not over. On the west coast of Africa, children are still sold as slaves for the price of a few bags of rice. In countries like Benin, Christian organizations run homes for children who have been kidnapped and used as slaves, or forced to serve as child soldiers. Some have scars from beatings and torture.

Children stolen or sold as slaves in Africa are often routed through Europe on their way to be sold to slave-holders in Arab nations. There are an estimated two hundred human smuggling organizations operating in Turkey alone. In the year 2000, dozens of abandoned ships filled with slaves — children who had been left to starve or to drown — were found by maritime authorities in Turkish waters.

As Christians, we can pray and support organizations like Mercy Ships, World Vision, and Samaritan's Purse, that are helping these children. And, like Millie Keith, we should keep our eyes open and learn the truth, so that we can speak for those who cannot speak for themselves.

KEITH FAMILY TREE

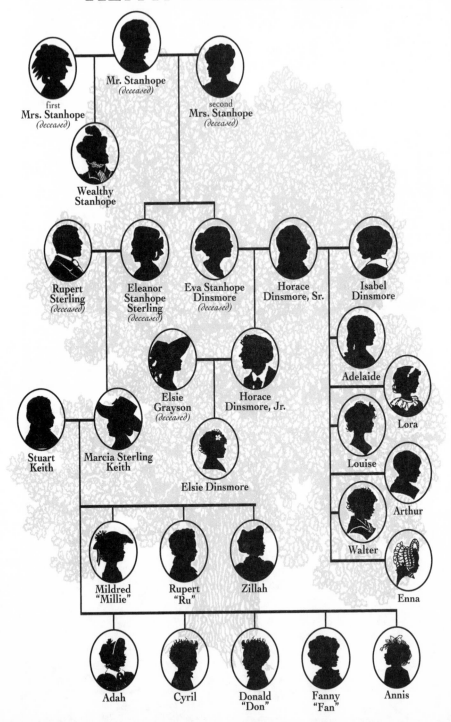

SETTING

$\mathcal{O}$ur story begins in October of 1836 in Pleasant Plains, Indiana, a young frontier town where the Keith family has lived and worked for three years.

CHARACTERS IN
PLEASANT PLAINS, INDIANA

∞ THE KEITH FAMILY ∞

Stuart Keith — the father of the Keith family; a respected attorney-at-law.

Marcia Keith — the mother of the Keith family and the step-niece of Aunt Wealthy Stanhope.

The Keith children:

> **Mildred Eleanor ("Millie")** — age 15
> **Rupert ("Ru")** — age 14
> **Zillah** — age 12
> **Adah** — age 11
> **Cyril** and **Donald ("Don")** — age 10, twin boys
> **Fanny ("Fan")** — age 8
> **Annis** — age 4

Wealthy Stanhope — a woman in her late 50s; Marcia's step-aunt who raised her from infancy; step-aunt to Horace Dinsmore, Jr.; she lives in Lansdale, Ohio.

∾ Friends in Pleasant Plains ∾

Mrs. Prior — the landlady of the Union Hotel.

Mrs. Lightcap — a widow whose deceased husband was the town's blacksmith; she now runs the local stagecoach stop (way station).

> **Gordon** — age 19
>
> **Rhoda Jane** — age 17
>
> **Emmaretta** — age 11
>
> **Minerva ("Min")** — age 10

Dr. and Mrs. Chetwood — the town physician and his wife.

> **William ("Bill")** — age 17
>
> **Claudina** — age 16

Mr. and Mrs. Grange — the bank president and his wife.

> **Lucilla ("Lu")** — age 17
>
> **Teddy** — age 12

Mr. and Mrs. Monocker — the owner of the local mercantile store and his wife.

> **York** — age 19
>
> **Helen** — age 18

Mr. and Mrs. Ormsby — a local businessman and his wife.

> **Wallace** — age 18
>
> **Sally** — age 8

Mr. and Mrs. Roe — local farmers.

> **Beth** — age 17

Reverend Matthew and **Celestia Ann Lord** — a local minister and his wife.

Damaris Drybread — a local teacher, age 25.

Mrs. Prescott — a widowed neighbor.
> **Effie** — age 10

Nicholas Ransquate — a local young man, age 28.

Maxine and **Monique Claxton** — the daughters of the local barber.

CHARACTERS AT
ROSELANDS PLANTATION

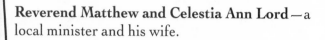 THE DINSMORE HOUSEHOLD

Horace Dinsmore, Sr. — uncle to Marcia Keith.

Isabel Dinsmore — wife of Horace Dinsmore, Sr.

The Dinsmore children:
> **Adelaide** — age 12
> **Lora** — age 10
> **Louise** — age 8
> **Arthur** — age 6
> **Walter** — age 4
> **Enna** — age 2

Miss Worth — governess to the Dinsmore children.

Mrs. Brown — the housekeeper at Roselands.

Jonati—a slave; nursemaid to the Dinsmore children.

Laylie—a slave girl, age 10.

Luke—a slave and Laylie's brother, age 15.

∞ OTHERS ∞

Otis Lochneer—a friend of the Dinsmores, age 19.

Mr. and Mrs. Landreth—a wealthy middle-aged couple.

Charles Landreth—nephew to the Landreths and a friend of the Dinsmore family, age 20.

Mrs. Travilla—owner of Ion Plantation; a friend of the Dinsmore family.

Old Rachel—an elderly slave woman belonging to Mrs. Travilla.

CHAPTER

1

The Last to Know

*Do you not know? Have
you not heard?*

ISAIAH 40:28

The Last to Know

*F*ifteen-year-old Millie Keith fought against the thistledown tickle in her chest, the little explosions of prickling in her lungs. She had walked too quickly on her way to the footbridge where the Kankakee Marsh joined the creek. She tried to take shallow breaths of the crisp morning air, but the cough came anyway, shaking her slight frame.

"It's not fair, Jesus!" Millie cried out loud. She wanted to run through the morning, taking great gulps of the autumn air and shouting praises. But instead, she leaned against the handrail, pressing her hand against her chest to ease the pain the coughing always brought. She had survived the terrible season of ague two years before, but the fever had left her weakened, and that winter a racking cough had set in. The second winter she had been little more than an invalid, confined to her bedroom or the couch in the sitting room. "Her lungs are not yet healed," Dr. Chetwood had said. "A change of climate is necessary. Another winter here . . ." His voice had trailed off.

Stuart and Marcia Keith, Millie's parents, had determined that although a change of climate was necessary, it was quite impossible. The cost of sending Millie away for months was beyond their means. Aunt Wealthy had offered to take Millie in, inviting her to come and stay in Lansdale for the winter, but Ohio's climate was just as harsh as Indiana's. Besides, there was still the insurmountable cost of the journey.

Now, winter was coming again, and Millie could see the worry in her Mamma's eyes, and several times she caught

3

her Pappa looking at her with a wrinkle on his brow. Millie drew a deep breath, and exhaled carefully. "I wouldn't leave," she said aloud, "even if I had somewhere to go. Mamma needs me."

Suddenly, Joshua 1:9 popped into Millie's head. She shook her long braids as if to shake off the thought. *How odd. That isn't even my memory verse. It's John 1 that I'm to teach on at Bible study this morning.* "I wouldn't leave," she repeated with even more conviction.

Once upon a time, Millie had dreaded moving to the frontier, leaving the parties, fine gowns, and society of her friends in Lansdale, Ohio. But in the three years they had lived in Pleasant Plains, Indiana, Millie had changed and Pleasant Plains had changed too. Strangers had been transformed into dear friends. People who had never heard the Gospel before had come to know Jesus and love Him. The Keiths had been good for Pleasant Plains, and the frontier had been good for the Keiths. They had become a mix of the old and the new—the pleasant manners and gentle ways of the society of Lansdale, and the courage, strength, and independence of the frontier.

Millie paused to take in the changing colors of the Kankakee. It was true that the fevers did come off the swamp in the stagnant summer air, but there was something indescribably sweet about the wildness and solitude of the marsh. Millie felt the steadfastness of God's love when she sat in Ru's rose garden, and she felt like shouting His praise when she walked alone in the marsh. She had fallen in love with the Kankakee in all its seasons, and had learned its hills and pools almost as well as Rhoda Jane and Gordon Lightcap knew them.

On an impulse, Millie set her bookbag down, kicked off her brogans, and wiggled her stockinged toes. She couldn't run, but she could climb. She pulled herself up onto the flat handrail. Her petticoats made climbing awkward, but once she was on her feet, she walked confidently — toe-to-heel, arms wide for balance — to the very center of the bridge, and then stood admiring the view. The marsh landscape was never the same two days in a row. Even the blue of the sky changed. Now, in early October, the sky was light blue. This afternoon it would hum with jewel-winged dragonflies hovering over the surface of the waters. The wildness of it all seeped into her like the warmth of the sun, filling her with joy. "For behold," she shouted, throwing her arms wide, "He who forms the mountains, creates the wind, and reveals his thoughts to man, he who turns dawn to darkness, and treads the high places of the earth — the Lord God Almighty is his name!"

"You are a strange girl, Millie Keith."

Millie almost toppled backwards into the stream as she spun around to see who had spoken. Nicholas Ransquate was leaning against the rail. Posed against the rail was a better description. His pantaloons, gaiters, and white shirt were impeccable. There was a deep red bachelor's button tucked in the lapel of his coat, and his hat was perched at a jaunty angle on his balding dome. Millie shook her head. "Hello, Mr. Ransquate."

Nicholas reached up in a silent offer of assistance. Millie bit her lip. Climbing up onto the rail while no one was watching was one thing. Getting down in any decent fashion with a gentleman present was quite another. She could hardly refuse the offer, so taking the proffered hand in one of hers, and gathering her skirts in the other so they would not billow, she jumped down off the rail. "I hardly find it strange to exalt the Lord on such a wondrous morning," she asserted.

"Most young ladies of your age would be quite content to do so from the safety of terra firma," Nicholas said. "They would forgo perching like penguins atop a railing. How old are you now, Millie?"

"Penguins do not perch," Millie corrected, ignoring his question. Millie glanced sideways at him and then looked away quickly. *Is that a new hat?* she wondered. *Surely not.*

Nicholas Ransquate was twenty-eight years of age — and determined to find a wife. He had made it his custom to speak to every girl in Pleasant Plains on or about her sixteenth birthday, the respectable age for engagement. Everyone could tell when a proposal was coming; Nicholas always bought himself a new hat for the occasion. The local haberdasher had experienced very profitable times in the last three years as Millie's friends had, one by one, dashed the poor man's hopes of wedded bliss.

"Like a robin, then," Nicholas laughed, but his face grew somber as Millie struggled against a coughing fit. "You must learn not to exert yourself," he said, as she tried to put her shoes back on without exposing too much stocking. "If you won't take care for your own sake, then take care out of consideration for those who would be hurt if you should come to any harm."

Millie managed to wiggle her feet into the sturdy shoes. "Good day, Mr. Ransquate," she said. "I really must be going. I have to teach the ladies' Bible study today, and I fear I will be late." She started walking quickly.

Poor Nicholas worked very hard at his proposals, and he always entered into them with the greatest hopes and dreams. As far as anyone could tell, he used the same proposal again and again—under the impression perhaps that practice makes perfect—only refining and expanding it to suit the lady. It had taken him a full thirty minutes to propose to Rhoda Jane. But by the time he had proposed to Lucilla Grange, it was forty-five. Helen Monocker had assured Millie that, left uninterrupted—and Nicholas was hard to interrupt—the next girl could expect to listen to him for a full hour.

"Let me carry your bag," he said, taking the bag from her and hurrying after her. "I've heard disturbing news, and there's something important I must talk to you about before . . ."

Something important? Millie flushed and started walking quickly, but just as she reached the end of the footbridge, she had to stop and cough again. She caught a flash of red hair through the bushes as she straightened up. "Cyril and Don Keith!" she called hopefully. "Are you hiding in those bushes?"

Cyril and Don stepped out. Cyril's overalls were rolled up almost to his knees, and he had a bait bucket in one hand and a fishing pole in the other. His freckles had almost tanned away, but his red hair was as bright as ever. The small creature that followed tamely at Cyril's heels could have been mistaken for a large black cat—if one overlooked the white stripe that divided it from nose to tail.

Nicholas stepped behind Millie, then realized what he had done and stepped back again. "I will never get used to the sight of that creature following your brothers around."

"Ambrosia ain't bad," Don said as he bent to scratch the skunk's ears, " 'cept she don't like hound dogs."

"Nor people *we* don't like walkin' with our sister," added Cyril, eyeing Nicholas closely.

"I . . . umm. It has been delightful, Millie," said Nicholas. "We must talk soon." He returned the bookbag to her, bowed, and hurried back across the bridge.

"Hello, Ambrosia," Millie said, stooping to pet the skunk. "You need to work on your truth-telling, Don. And you, too, Cyril. Poor Ambrosia doesn't spray anyone at all."

"We didn't say she was going to spray anyone," Don said. "I just said she don't like hound dogs."

Josiah Weaver, the young circuit rider who owned Ambrosia, had sworn to the Keiths that she was defense-less — incapable of spraying at all. When the ferryman had refused to let the preacher's pet cross the river with him, Josiah had paid Cyril a dollar to keep her until he returned in a month. Marcia said no, of course, until Josiah explained that he'd rescued the creature from a group of boys intent on stoning her to death, and she was very dear to him. Marcia had taken pity on the young preacher, and said one month couldn't hurt. That had been a year ago, and there had been no sign that the skunk could spray. Neither had there been any sign of Josiah Weaver.

"Hmmm," sighed Millie as she straightened up. "Now what are you two doing hiding in the bushes?" she asked suspiciously.

"We got us a money-payin' job, that's what," Cyril said, hitching up his overalls.

"Really? Who's paying you to fish?" she asked.

"We ain't fishin', Millie," Don began, but Cyril elbowed him.

"What are you doing, then?"

Cyril's eyebrows went up and his lips clamped shut. Millie knew it was pointless to ask him, so she addressed the question directly to Don. "What are you doing?"

"Wallace Ormsby is payin' us two bits a week to watch over you an' tell him if you go walkin' out with any young men."

Millie felt her cheeks burn for the second time this morning. Wallace was studying law under her father. At eighteen he looked every inch the gentleman, but sometimes she felt he acted more like her younger brother Ru. "You can tell Wallace from me that he is wasting his money. I am not 'walking out' with any young man," said Millie.

"Now, why would we go an' do that?" Cyril's face screwed up. "I figure we'll get a bonus for chasin' ol' Ransquate away!"

"Cyril!"

"Never mind, Millie," Don said, giving his twin a look. "We're not gonna tell Wallace about that. Come on, I'll carry your bag."

Millie started through town, escorted by two raggle-taggle redheads and a skunk. Pleasant Plains had grown since the stagecoach line had come to town. New shops were opening each year—a haberdasher, supported largely by Mr. Ransquate; a dressmaker, with yards of material displayed in the window; a barber, Mr. Claxton, who also extracted teeth and sold patent medicine; and a print shop, which had opened near Stuart Keith's law office. Wallace looked up from his desk as they walked by, and waved. Millie put her chin up and ignored him. *Paying my brothers to spy on me indeed!* she thought to herself, disgusted.

The street was quiet at this time of the morning, empty save for Mrs. Lightcap, who was standing on the street corner engaged in an animated conversation with a post.

"Who's she talkin' to, Millie?" Don asked.

"Her dead man," Cyril said. "Same as always."

Millie's Remarkable Journey

"Hush," Millie said. It was true that when Mrs. Lightcap's mind wandered, she had long conversations with her dead husband. But on most days she was perfectly competent to sort the mail that came in on the stage, and to help Rhoda Jane serve meals to the passengers.

"Good morning, Mrs. Lightcap," Millie said. Mrs. Lightcap turned slightly puzzled eyes to Millie.

"Millie, I almost missed you," she said. "He'll be along any moment, and I wanted to say goodbye. You will tell Rhoda Jane I said goodbye? Tell her to take care of Min and Emmaretta until I get back."

"Where are you going?"

"New York, of course! He'll be here soon, and we must get to New York."

"Why don't you wait inside with a nice cup of tea?" Millie suggested.

"Tea would be lovely, dear," Mrs. Lightcap said. Millie took her arm and led her to the boardwalk, and then to the Union Hotel. Cyril and Don followed along at a safe distance.

"She's having another spell, eh?" Mrs. Prior said, when Millie led Mrs. Lightcap in. "Poor dear. Cyril and Don!" The boys jumped. "Get that critter out of here! What kind of a hotel do you think I am running here?"

"Bye, Millie," Cyril called as they dodged out the door. "See you at home!" They ran up the street, Ambrosia a black streak behind them.

"They didn't get my sugar, did they?" Mrs. Prior asked suspiciously, tipping the bowl on the table to check. "I don't mean to imply anything about your brothers, but *someone* has been taking sugar lumps right out of the bowl for the last few weeks. We'll just let Mrs. Lightcap sit here for a spell. It's nice weather for travelin', ain't it?"

"I suppose so," Millie said. "Maybe that's why she thinks she's going to New York. Thank you for watching her. I'll let Rhoda Jane know where she is when I get to the Bible study. Oh dear! I am going to be late!"

"You go right on," Mrs. Prior said. "And tell Rhoda Jane to stop by on her way home."

The Young Ladies Bible Society had already gathered in the gracious sitting room at the Monockers when Millie arrived. Helen and Lu, Rhoda Jane, Effie Prescott, Celestia Ann Lord, Damaris Drybread, Claudina Chetwood, Maxine and Monique Claxton, the barber's daughters, and Beth Roe were seated in their places. The buzz of conversation stopped as Millie came into the room. *Of all the days to be late!*

"I apologize for my tardiness," Millie said, hoping no one would have time to ask why she was late. This was the wrong time and place to bring up Nicholas Ransquate's new hat. "Let's begin in prayer." She bowed her head. "Lord, help us focus on Your Word and Your ways. Help us not to be afraid to hear the truth, or to act on it." She could hear the rustle of silk skirts as she prayed. "In Jesus' name. Amen."

Millie cleared her throat and started again, fighting the prickles in her chest. "Jesus said that we are to be a light on a hill. Doesn't a light challenge the darkness? He said that we are to be the salt of the earth. Doesn't salt alter the flavor of a food? If the world around us goes on just as if we did not exist, then we are not living as Jesus intended us to. We are supposed to change the world!" said Millie. "I prayed for a long time about what to teach today, and I finally decided that I had to speak about something that

tears at my heart—and must break God's heart even more."
All eyes were on her as she continued. "I would like to read
a letter from a gentleman planter in Tennessee. This letter
was published in last February's issue of the *Liberator.*"

Someone groaned, but when Millie glanced up, there was
no clue as to who it had been. She wished she had a more
recent copy of the paper to read from, but the abolitionist
paper had stopped arriving in the mail the first week of
March. Millie was unsure whether the paper was even published any longer. The town's newspaper, the *Pleasant Plains
Crier,* carried almost no editorials about slavery. *Lord, help me
be bold*, Millie prayed silently, as she took the *Liberator* from
her bag and opened to a letter on the second page.

> *This year I have made the painful decision to send my
> young sons to New York to be educated. I have decided on this
> distressing plan of action because I feel there is no hope of raising
> them in decency here. There is not one attractive black girl in
> this state who is not the concubine of a white man. I have no
> intention of impugning the character of the girls—slaves have no
> choice in these matters, you see. The practice of amalgamation
> is not occasional or general. It is universal. There is not an old
> plantation in the state where the grandchildren of the owner are
> not whipped in the fields.*

"I don't understand," Lu Grange said. "Why would the
owner allow his grandchildren to be in the fields? Surely
the slaves . . ."

"The grandchildren the writer refers to *are* slaves,"
Rhoda Jane Lightcap explained. "The writer is speaking of
the grandchildren of the owner and his slave mistresses.
That's what amalgamation is."

"I don't believe it!" Lu said. "That is pure fabrication, and that . . . paper has no business being read in a ladies Bible study! It's . . . it's indecent!"

"Slavery is indecent," Millie said. "That's my point. Our text for today is John 1:12–13." She opened her tattered Bible carefully. The book was ragged from constant wear. The pages had been stained with tears, shaken with laughter, and endured at least one cup of hot chocolate spilt in the book of Lamentations, but Millie's fingers knew each and every book, and many verses, by feel. " 'Yet to all who received him, to those who believed in his name, he gave the right to become children of God—children born not of natural descent, nor of human decision or a husband's will, but born of God.' Now if everyone who is a Christian is a child of God, that would make the Christian slaves our brothers and sisters."

Lu Grange was waving her hand. "Yes, Lu?" said Millie.

"I don't think my mother approves of me discussing slavery. In fact, I'm sure she does not. Politics, slavery, and war are fine for men to discuss. But they are so . . . unladylike, don't you think? And I know she wouldn't let me read those papers."

"Those abolitionist papers lie, anyway," Helen said. "Slave owners are people just like you and me."

"Not like me," Millie said firmly. "I would never own another human being!"

Helen shrugged. "Nobody will force you to. But what gives you the right to make that decision for others? My father agrees with his friend, Congressman James Henry Hammond of South Carolina: 'Slavery is the greatest of all the great blessings which a kind Providence has bestowed upon the South.' " Helen was quoting now, and using her voice to good dramatic effect. Millie could almost imagine the congressman standing behind her, his hand over his heart, saying, "Domestic slavery produces the highest toned, the purest, best organization of society that has ever existed on the face of the earth!"

"Tripe!" Rhoda Jane Lightcap exclaimed with her usual grace and aplomb. She snatched the paper from Millie's hands and turned to an example of the advertisements published in the southern papers: " 'Reward: for the return of Jessie, a female slave, age sixteen. I tried to brand her face and thigh with a letter M, but it didn't come out good on her face, so she may wear a bonnet to try to hide it. . . . If caught, return to John Martin, Tennessee.' I somehow doubt that Jessie feels this is a blessing of Providence," said Rhoda Jane with firmness.

Helen laughed. "I could write those fictitious ads myself. They mean nothing. Millie, your own cousin brought a personal slave with him when he came to visit. They seemed to be very fond of one another. And you must admit that slavery is fully supported by the Bible."

"I admit no such thing," Millie said. "Angelina Grimke proves conclusively that . . . "

Several of the girls interrupted her. "Not Grimke again!" they groaned.

Millie had first heard of Angelina Grimke when her name appeared on a letter to William Lloyd Garrison, the editor of the *Liberator*, the year before. Angelina Grimke claimed to have grown up in South Carolina, the daughter of a wealthy slaveholding family. Millie was impressed with her plea to end slavery and her firsthand descriptions of the pain and degradation it caused. Aunt Wealthy then sent Millie a slim volume entitled *Appeal to the Christian Women of the South*. The pamphlet was a well-reasoned, compelling argument against slavery, using the Bible as its text and appealing to the women of the South to unite against it.

"I don't believe this 'Angelina' is a real person," Helen said. "She is the fabrication of a northern troublemaker. No lady would be as bold as she is claimed to be. They say she speaks in public meeting halls!"

"She is real! And slavery is a great evil! We must stand against it!" insisted Millie.

"How can we know for sure?" Effie Prescott asked in her quiet voice. "The southerners I have met seemed like kind and courteous people—like your cousin, Millie. I don't see how they could do the things we read about in these papers. We've never seen it ourselves. How are we supposed to know for sure if the awful stories we hear are true?"

"Millie will find out," Celestia Ann said with certainty. "That's how."

"I...will?" Millie questioned as she looked from one to the other.

"Of course you will," Celestia Ann said. "You can't spend four months on a cotton plantation without seeing for yourself! You will write to us, won't you?"

"What are you talking about?" Millie's head was spinning. "I'm not going anywhere!"

Everyone looked at Lu.

"I thought you knew, Millie," she said, flushing. "Everybody else knows."

"What do they know, and how do they know it?" Millie asked, gripping her Bible.

Lu replied, "I heard Mrs. Lightcap reading the letter aloud to Mrs. Ormsby."

"What letter?" Millie asked, trying to control her temper. "What did it say?"

Millie's Remarkable Journey

"That you are going to Roselands Plantation," Effie volunteered.

"To visit your mother's relations," Lu continued. "You will stay for the winter months."

Exasperated, Millie responded, "Is there anything else I should know?"

"The cotton crop is progressing well, your cousins are shopping in Philadelphia, and Enna has a slight cold."

"Who's Enna?" Monique asked.

"My baby cousin," Millie said between clenched teeth.

"Oh, I hope she feels better!" exclaimed Monique.

"Promise that you will write us the truth," Effie said. "We trust you, Millie. Promise that you will."

The Bible study meeting came to a quick close.

"Bible Study is always so . . . interesting when you teach," remarked Claudina as she said goodbye to Millie and Rhoda Jane. "We will all be praying for you, Millie."

"I am sorry, Millie," Rhoda Jane said as they walked down the street together. "I thought you knew, too. Mother doesn't usually read the mail. It was one of her bad days, and the letter was posted in New York. She thought it was from my father. They were in the theater there. She was so excited."

"She thinks he's coming back for her," Millie said. "I left her at the Union Hotel."

"Oh! Thank you," said Rhoda Jane, turning away and starting toward the Union.

"Wait!" Millie grabbed her friend's arm. "I know it's not her fault, really. But it's 1836, for heavens sake! Couldn't *someone* invent a contraption that would keep a person's correspondence from the eyes of any casual reader?"

16

CHAPTER

2

Stranger in a Strange Land

The Lord replied, "My Presence will go with you, and I will give you rest."

EXODUS 33:14

"oselands! Mamma, how could you?" Millie said, dropping her bonnet on the couch.

"Oh, Millie." Marcia stood and took her daughter in her arms. "I had no idea that you would hear. I only just received the letter from Horace myself."

"It's not that, Mamma. I know you couldn't help what Mrs. Lightcap did. *She* can't even help it. It's just . . . I don't want to go. Who will help you with the sewing and the cooking?"

"Adah and Zillah are quite old enough to help," Marcia said. "And even Fan is helping with the chores and watching Annis." She tipped Millie's face up. "Don't you know that your Pappa and I love you? We have prayed and prayed, and this is the best answer we have. Another winter here . . . Millie, we don't want to lose you. The milder climate of the South will strengthen your lungs."

"Isn't God able to look out for me?"

"Yes, He is," Marcia said. "Your Pappa and I believe He has provided a way. We had been praying about sending you to a milder climate for the cold months, but we did not know where, or how we would find the money. Then my Uncle Horace wrote that he would like to repay me for the kindness I showed him and Cousin Horace when my Aunt Eva, his first wife, died. He offered to let you stay with him and study with his own children. I understand they have an excellent governess and music teacher. And Uncle Horace himself is coming here to escort you on the journey."

"When is he coming, Mamma?"

Millie's Remarkable Journey

"He could be here any day. My letter caught up with him in New York, where he had traveled on business."

Millie sighed. How could she bear to leave her beloved Mamma and Pappa and the children? Yet the prickles in her lungs told her she had no real choice.

That night, Millie studied the faces of her family around the supper table. Zillah was becoming a young lady—as old as Millie herself had been when they moved to Pleasant Plains. Adah was just one year behind. Mamma was right. They were old enough to cook and sew and clean, and they kept after their lessons with Mamma and Pappa. Fan could watch over baby Annis; Ru, Cyril, and Don tended the gardens and the animals. Even Annis, who had just turned four, helped with the chores. *They can manage without me. But can I manage without them? The last time I made a journey, it was with my family around me, and I was responsible for watching over my little brothers and sisters. This time I will be . . . alone. Or at the very least, staying with a family I know nothing about.*

"Will they take the stage the whole way?" Ru asked, for no one could talk of anything but Millie's coming journey.

"I expect they will travel by stage and by boat," Marcia said. "And possibly by rail car, depending on the route Uncle Horace chooses."

"By steam locomotive!" Ru looked at her, and Millie knew he could barely contain his envy. The walls of Ru's room were covered with schematics for steam locomotives: the *Rocket*, the *Agenoria*, and the *Stourbridge Lion*. Ru could describe the finer points of each. "It will be a light one, no doubt. The American tracks can't bear the weight of a monster like the British *Agenoria*. But she'll still burn four tons of coal in an hour, I'll wager."

Marcia frowned. "You will do no such thing, Rupert Keith. Gambling is a vice."

"You will travel through Philadelphia," Zillah said dreamily. "Think of the shops!"

"Are you sure it's proper for her to travel alone, Mamma?" Adah asked, looking from her mother to her father hopefully. "Perhaps we should all go."

"She will not be alone," replied Marcia. "And we cannot afford a trip this year. Cyril, stop feeding that skunk under the table. Ambrosia will be allowed to dine with this family the day she can use a fork and a spoon, and not before."

Cyril fished his pet from under the table and carried her out of the room. The conversation went on pleasantly throughout the meal. Finally, Stuart folded his linen napkin and set it on the table. "Will you take a walk with your parents, Millie, dear? Let the girls clean up."

Millie hurried to her room for a warm shawl, and then joined them on the porch. She took her Pappa's arm on one side, and her Mamma's on the other.

"Where are we going?"

"Just going," Stuart said.

They stopped in the barn to pet the velvet noses of Inspiration and Glory, the two saddle mares the Keiths had purchased the year before. While everything in Pleasant Plains was close enough to walk to, Stuart had clients in nearby towns that he sometimes needed to visit. Stuart may have purchased the horses for business, but Millie loved riding for riding's sake. If she were feeling too weak for a long walk, she could saddle Inspiration and be gone for half a day. "Fan will take good care of you while I'm gone," Millie told the horse. Inspiration had proved not only a dependable saddle horse, but also a good baby-sitter. Fan would stay on her wide, bare back for hours. Millie had even found her sister fast asleep on the horse, her little fingers twined in its mane.

Glory, on the other hand, was a jumper. She was fun to ride, but impossible to keep fenced in. The boys seemed to spend half of their time chasing her, and the other half riding her madly through the marsh. Glory tossed her head and ran her rubbery lips up Millie's arm looking for a carrot or a lump of maple sugar.

"Do you think there will be horses at Roselands?" asked Millie.

"The Dinsmores keep a very fine stable," Marcia said. "Or, at least they did when I visited many years ago."

They said goodbye to the horses and continued down the hill through the twilight, arm in arm. Stuart loved walking, and they talked or stopped and laughed about many of the places they passed.

Stuart paused to admire Lightcap's Stables that stood just below the Big Yellow House—the house they had lived in when they first moved to Pleasant Plains. "Now that is a good piece of work," he said, admiring the stable building. Millie smiled. She should have known. Her Pappa was very attached to the place. After Gordon had almost destroyed his hand in an accident, Stuart had spent weeks helping at the stable, shoveling stalls, throwing hay, brushing horses—and talking to Gordon Lightcap, who had just become a Christian.

The Big Yellow House itself had been converted into a first-rate way station—a stage stop with neat, clean rooms and food prepared by Rhoda Jane. Even now, music and light were spilling out of the windows. The travelers who had arrived on the stage had eaten a good dinner cooked up by Rhoda Jane, and now Mrs. Lightcap was playing her

piano as they gathered in the great room of the inn. Her
rich contralto voice was rippling through "Oh, What a
Charming City," a song about New York. A few voices
joined in. Millie's fingers twitched, imagining the smooth
ivory keys. She had spent many afternoons at Rhoda Jane's
since the Lightcaps had purchased the piano.

"Ah! A lively tune," Stuart said, bowing to Marcia. "I
believe we have met here before. Would you care to dance?"

"Stuart, I . . . !" Marcia began, but before she could finish
the sentence, he scooped her up and spun her around the stable yard. Millie laughed as their waltz somehow became a
polka. Stuart finally stopped, breathless, and looked down at
his bride. "And what do you say to that, my dear?"

Marcia gazed up at him lovingly. "I think," she said, "that
I am standing in a fresh cow pie—in my second best shoes!"

Stuart looked down at her feet. "Gadzooks! Who let the
cows into the ballroom?" He picked her up and carried her
to the wooden steps of the stable. Millie helped clean the
shoes with handfuls of hay, laughing the whole time. When
the shoes were recovered, Stuart sat down on the wooden
steps beside Marcia and Millie.

"So, you are about to set out on a great adventure,
daughter," he said, stretching out his legs and leaning back
on his elbows. "Do you remember a conversation we had
here once, a long, long time ago?"

"Not so long ago, Pappa," Millie said. "Two and a half
years. I asked you how you know when you're in love."

"And I asked for a few years to think about it. Of course,
when I said that, I had no idea you would grow into a beautiful young lady so quickly." Stuart sighed, and then continued, "Are there any young men in Pleasant Plains that it . . .
pains you to leave?"

Millie's Remarkable Journey

"None that I would allow to waltz me into a cow pie," Millie said, smiling. "Wallace is one of my best friends, and Gordon Lightcap too, but I am not in love with either of them."

Stuart nodded. "I didn't think so. Poor Wallace will be disappointed, I fear. And I hear that Nicholas has purchased a new hat."

"Pappa!" cried Millie.

"Don't worry, I would never approve. Would you like me to speak to him?"

"I . . . I was hoping to avoid him altogether," Millie said, "and planning to pray fervently for him to find a wife while I am gone. There must be someone who would love to marry Nicholas . . . I do feel sorry for him, Pappa."

"Yes," Stuart said. "Ahem. Now, as I was saying, since you are going off on an adventure, I thought it was time that we finished that talk."

"So you have figured it all out, then? You seemed a bit taken aback last time," said Millie, lightheartedly.

"Of course I haven't," he said seriously. "That's why I brought your mother along. Go ahead, dear! I'll jump right in with anything I can think of."

"I hardly think it's necessary, Mamma," Millie said. "I don't intend to fall in love for years and years, at least. Maybe never at all. I might just live like Aunt Wealthy, doing anything I choose."

"Good," Marcia said. "Then for years and years, you can practice exactly what your Aunt Wealthy told me to practice when I was your age. I know it will be of value no matter what you decide about romance. First, honor God in all you do. Second, give your heart to Jesus."

24

"Mamma! You know I asked Jesus into my heart when I was a little girl!"

"And we're proud of the way you have been living for Him. But that's not what I meant. Long ago, before I met your father, I prayed, 'Jesus, please hold my heart in Your hands. Don't let me give it or any piece of it away. I want YOU to give it away in Your time, to the right person. Please hold it tight, lock it up, and keep the key.' And He did. He kept my heart safe for your Pappa."

"That was a very good thing," Stuart said. "If God had not given me your Mamma's heart, I could never have won it. There were handsome young men lined up around the block, their hearts pinned on their sleeves, waiting for your Mamma. Young men with money, young men with good looks . . . one even had a ukulele. He used to sing outside her window. What was his name?"

"Marshal P. Livingstone. His father owned a fleet of ships. He was good-looking, and had a very nice voice, too," said Marcia.

"There was musically gifted and nautical Marshal P. Livingstone, rich as Midas and good-looking to boot. And then there was me—a skinny law student with nothing but a Bible and a winsome, charming smile. Of course, I did have a great deal of talent. And a keen legal mind. Tell me, my dear, why did you, a lovely heiress, choose a penniless student of law?"

Marcia folded her arms and looked up at him. "It must have been your humility. It certainly couldn't have been your dancing!"

Millie laughed, and a cough racked through her body. She tried to hold it in, but could not, and leaned against the fence until the coughing fit was done.

Stuart and Marcia exchanged a worried look. "This is the right thing to do, Millie," said Marcia.

"But Mamma, into the southern states?"

"I know. Remember, I traveled to Roselands once, too. I like your Uncle Horace very much, and respect many things about him. He is a moral man, and even attends church. But I'm afraid he has no personal relationship with Jesus. Your uncle would not consider himself a cruel man, but slaveholding is not an occupation that lends itself to Christian ways. And I have never met his new wife. If you were not a strong Christian, and strong-minded as well, we would have a much harder time letting you go, even for only four months."

"Sometimes I don't feel very strong," Millie said. "What will I do without both of you?"

"Do you remember the Fifth Commandment?" Marcia asked softly.

"Of course," Millie said. "Honor your father and mother. It's the first commandment with a promise attached—'so that you may live long in the land the Lord your God is giving you.'"

"That's what you are to do," Marcia said. "Whether you are at home, or far away. Honor your parents."

"I've always thought that meant much more than just respecting your parents," Stuart said. "I believe it means bringing them honor by the way you act and by the decisions you make. We know you will honor us in your actions and decisions, no matter where you are. We are very proud of you, Millie."

Tears came to Millie's eyes. She started to cough, but managed to hold it in.

"Now, we need to get you home," Marcia said. "The air is getting crisp, Stuart."

That night as Millie prepared for bed, she savored the homeyness of her room. Her long white nightgown was warm enough, but her room was chilly. Static electricity crackled and sparked as she straightened her long blonde hair with a bristle brush. The hair seemed to have a mind of its own, trying to rise into the air and cling to the brush. It never acted this way in the summer — only in the fall and winter when the air was cool and dry, and before her cough got really bad. Millie finally managed to tame her hair into braids, and then sat down at her writing desk and turned up her lamp. She picked up her diary, practically the thickness of a novel, and thumbed through the pages.

The very first page had a prayer list pasted to it that she had started when she was thirteen. She smiled as she ran her finger over the names. *Rhoda Jane Lightcap, Damaris Drybread.* Rhoda Jane had become a Christian after her name was inked here; Damaris had learned how to love. *Elsie Dinsmore.* Uncle Horace was grandfather to this young second cousin. His son, Horace Jr., had married very young, and when his wife died, he had never even gone to see his baby girl. Millie prayed for Elsie and Elsie's pappa every day, as she prayed for her own family and friends, but she had no way of knowing how God was answering those prayers. Surely if He were faithful to answer her prayers for people in Pleasant Plains, He would not leave Elsie all alone. Millie was eager for news of the little girl for whom she had prayed so long, but Millie knew it was a tender subject with the Dinsmores, and she would wait for Uncle Horace to bring it up.

27

Millie's Remarkable Journey

Millie continued to flip through the diary, past pages on which she'd written her daily reflections, prayers, answers to prayer, Scripture passages that held special meaning to her, goals and dreams, and other notes, until she reached a blank page. Then she dipped her steel-tipped pen in the inkwell, shook the excess ink off the end, and wrote out her mother's prayer. "Jesus, please hold my heart in Your hands . . . ." She spoke it earnestly to the Lord as the pen moved, and made it her own by signing it with a flourish: *Millie Keith, October 8, 1836.* She thought for a moment, then added, "P.S. Please help Nicholas Ransquate find a wife. Surely there must be someone who could love him." She shook her head, and marked the last sentence out, and replaced it with, "Bring someone who will love him." Then after further reflection, she wrote, "P.P.S. I am scared of leaving, scared of being on my own. Who will I talk to? What is Uncle Horace like? What is the truth about slavery? What if I *have* been believing lies? Help me to trust You, Lord, and not worry Mamma and Pappa by seeming to be afraid."

Satisfied, she pressed blotting paper lightly on the page to soak up any extra ink, and then flipped back through the pages. How strange that she would be leaving this place that she had written so much about. She would miss the winter social and Christmas with her family. A letter dated January 1836 caught her eye.

Dear God, You did a good job when You made snow. It muffles the world, hushes my thoughts, as if You are saying, "Be quiet, be still, and listen to Me." Oh Lord, I want to hear Your voice every day. Sometimes I hear it when I read my Bible. Sometimes I hear it in Your creation. Often I hear it in the words of my parents. Help me to listen, and never miss what You are saying to me. Awaken my ears to listen like one being taught, as it says in Isaiah 50:4.

Stranger in a Strange Land

Millie sat back and reflected on her day. *Has God spoken to me today? More than once, I'm sure. What was that Scripture that popped into my head when I was praising on the bridge? Oh yes, it was Joshua 1:9.* She looked it up in her Bible. *"Have I not commanded you? Be strong and courageous. Do not be terrified; do not be discouraged, for the Lord your God will be with you wherever you go,"* she read silently. *Wherever I go. Even to Roselands. Even to the South.* Millie sighed. *Thank You, Jesus. I love You, and I know I can trust You. You are my Good Shepherd — wherever I go.*

Millie inked her pen again and wrote out Joshua 1:9 on a page of its very own.

CHAPTER

Traveling Light

*Therefore I tell you, do not worry
about your life, what you will
eat; or about your body, what
you will wear. Life is more
than food, and the body
more than clothes.*

LUKE 12:22–23

*M*illie set about her chores with special diligence the next morning, but each time she started a task, Zillah took over—eager to prove that she could be trusted with the responsibility. As a result, the work was done well before noon. Millie finally retreated to her room with nothing to do but check over once again the list of things she would need to take with her: clothing, bonnets, shoes, books. She felt sure they would have books at Roselands, but she wanted a few of her favorites to keep her company on the way. Everything was ready, waiting to be packed. She fingered a line of fine stitches on a pretty green and black silk gown she had sewn for fall. She had even made a lovely matching bonnet. Her wardrobe might be limited, but her clothes were stylish and well-fitted, and she felt a certain satisfaction at the quality of her work.

"It's a good thing you are the best seamstress in Pleasant Plains," Zillah said from the doorway. "You won't have to be ashamed of your clothes, even at Roselands."

Millie laughed. "What do you want to borrow now, little sister?" she asked.

Zillah opened her eyes wide. "Why, Mildred Keith! What makes you think I want to borrow a thing?"

"Oh, let's see . . . compliments, flattery." Millie ticked them off on her fingers as she went. "The fact that you always wear my clothes . . . what are you going to do when I take them with me?"

"Learn to be more diligent with my needle," sighed Zillah. "I know I have to work harder on it. About that blouse?"

Millie's Remarkable Journey

"You may borrow it. But I expect it back in good shape when I return."

"And just one skirt? And perhaps a bonnet . . . "

"No." Millie ushered her little sister out of the room and started to shut the door behind her.

"I don't want you to go, Millie," Zillah said suddenly.

"Don't worry," Millie said giving her a hug. "You will be borrowing my clothes again before you know it!"

⁓

Millie was in the kitchen brewing a pot of tea when Don wandered in. "Just saw Nicholas Ransquate," he announced.

"Really? And why should that concern me?" she asked.

"No per*tic*ular reason," Don said, picking an apple out of the bowl on the table. "Other'n the fact that he is headed up our drive wearin' a new hat, and carrying a bunch of flowers." Millie dropped the kettle. It landed squarely on the stove, but water splashed out of the spout, hissing into steam as it hit the hot surface. Millie jumped back, flustered.

"You want me to get my slingshot, Millie?" asked Don, protectively.

"Of course not!" She put her hand to her head. "I . . . I was just thinking that I needed to work on my art. I am going out. Right now." She turned back at the door. "Thank you, Don."

Millie quickly gathered her sketchbook and charcoal sticks. Maybe it wouldn't be too bad to spend her birthday away from home after all. She made her way down the hill toward the river, and followed it up to the mouth of the creek, turning east to follow the stream up into the marsh. She settled herself among the roots of a willow tree that still had half of its leaves, providing shade to a deep, still pool that was home to a family of muskrats. When she had found a comfortable spot, Millie took out her sketchbook and a stick of charcoal.

Before she had become sick, Millie had hardly noticed the small creatures around her because there was always work to occupy her hands. It was during the winter months, as she lay in bed, that she had first noticed the birds outside her window. Gordon Lightcap had built her a feeder to attract even more. Aunt Wealthy had sent along two volumes, *Birds of America* and *Ornithological Biography, An Account of the Habits of the Birds of the United States of America*, both by John James Audubon. The pictures in *Birds of America* were like nothing Millie had ever seen before, each bird rendered in brilliant color and in a life-like pose. The book was quite expensive, she was sure. If there was one worldly pleasure Aunt Wealthy was likely to indulge, it was her love of fine books. Millie kept her copy in the parlor, and the younger children were only allowed to look at it while she was present. The second volume consisted of text describing the habits of the birds, as well as the author's adventures while observing them. Throughout the long winter months, Millie delighted in identifying each new species that came to her feeder, and dreamt of wandering for miles through the wilderness with nothing but a knapsack and art supplies. When spring came, she followed the birds outside, and bird watching led her to the edges of the marsh. Soon she was exploring it with Rhoda Jane, learning the paths and watching the creatures with delight.

Now, Millie was determined to catch the marsh on paper, to remember the small creatures that were snuggled in their nests, waiting out the winter, and the dragonfly larvae that lay in the cold water beneath the ice, waiting for the sun to set them free. She would be back to the marsh in the spring, when the baby muskrats came out for their first swim after the long ice.

Millie sat quietly beside the pool, waiting for the waters to move. Soon she saw a ripple, and then a small brown head appeared. She held her breath as the small creature glided closer, its tail moving like a snake in the water behind it. Audubon drew pictures of birds he had killed and then posed with wires in a lifelike way. It allowed him to go into great detail, but Millie couldn't stand the thought of killing the creatures she drew. If she could draw quickly enough, perhaps she could capture enough details to remember them by.

Do other people have favorite parts of creation, Lord? Muskrats are one of my favorites. I'm glad You thought to include them! Her fingers started to move, sketching the shape of the ripples and the muskrat's nose. The muskrat disappeared, leaving a burst of bubbles behind. Millie looked at her paper and frowned. That wasn't quite it. She smudged the lines with her finger, but it didn't help.

She tried her hand with a mourning dove that cooperated wonderfully by taking a sand bath nearby. Millie spent two hours sketching beside the pool before she decided that Nicholas had probably given up and gone home.

Gordon Lightcap's wagon was in front of the house and Gordon himself was lifting a trunk from the wagon bed when Millie arrived.

"Good afternoon, Millie," he said, tipping his hat and smiling after he set the trunk down. "Have you been sketching again?"

"Trying," Millie confessed. "I am not satisfied with the result."

"Could I take a look?" he asked.

Millie opened the book to her picture of a muskrat. "I don't think I quite captured it."

Gordon studied the charcoal-smudged page. "Ummm." He rubbed his jaw. "Drowning squirrels are a little hard to capture," he said at last. "Particularly in that last desperate moment of life."

Millie slugged his arm. "It's a muskrat!"

"A muskrat," he said, squinting at the paper. "Oh, I see it! Could I borrow your charcoal?"

Millie fished a charcoal stick out of her apron pocket. Gordon reached for it awkwardly with his right hand. His middle fingers were stiffened into almost a claw, but he could still grip with his thumb and little finger. He took the charcoal between them, held one end against his palm and the other on the paper, made a few swift lines, and the muskrat emerged from Millie's smudges.

"How did you do that?" Millie demanded.

"It's easy. I see the muskrat God meant it to be—and that's what I draw." He flipped to her sketch of the dove.

"And what's this?" he asked. "A rabbit?"

Millie sighed. "Were you making a delivery?" she asked.

"Oh! I thought I told you! I just delivered your Uncle Horace. Rhoda Jane told me how you feel about leaving," he lowered his voice, "about going south. But Millie, you have to go. This is going to make you well. And that matters . . . a lot . . . to some people."

"Thank you, Gordon," Millie said. "For fixing the muskrat, I mean. And for wishing me well, too. I know God has a plan."

Millie's Remarkable Journey

Gordon ran his good hand through his hair and smiled before he put his cap back on his head. "You have problems, I can fix 'em," he said with a grin. "Remember that, Millie."

Millie found the greater part of her family in the parlor, listening attentively to a distinguished-looking middle-aged gentleman; only Cyril, Don, and Ru were missing. Millie had entered quietly, and she watched curiously to see what this uncle was like. He was of the same height as her Pappa, but the differences were marked. Pappa seemed relaxed and friendly, Uncle Horace stiff and formal. *Why, he has no laugh wrinkles—none at all.*

The gentleman was explaining, "I propose to spend a week with you, Marcia, if it is convenient and agreeable, and then briefly stop in Lansdale before returning to Philadelphia, where I deposited my family before my business trip."

"That would be convenient, agreeable, and welcome!" Marcia replied. "And how I envy you the visit with Aunt Wealthy!"

Uncle Horace's coat was spotless, despite his journey, and his boots had obviously been shined. He started to turn toward Millie, his movements as precise as those of a machine, and Millie looked away, hoping he had not noticed how closely she was observing him. Then, realizing he was addressing her, she turned back with a blush.

"This must be Millie Keith," he said, bowing. "Horace Jr. spoke a great deal about you. He said you had a keen mind and noble character."

"Cousin Horace was too kind, Uncle, I'm sure," Millie said, blushing even redder. "Though we did have many long conversations."

Just then, Ru came in from the gardens, his hands clean, but his brown hair sun-streaked and windblown.

"Ru," Stuart said, "this is your Uncle Horace Dinsmore. Uncle Horace, my eldest son, Rupert."

The two shook hands, Ru saying, "I'm glad to meet you, sir. Mother has spoken of you often. May I carry your valise to the guest room?"

Uncle Horace looked at Marcia, who nodded.

"Surely that can't be the Rupert you have written of!" Uncle Horace said, as Ru left the room. "I am afraid the gifts I brought may be altogether inappropriate. I came expecting children and I find a young woman," he bowed to Millie again, "and a full-grown man with the grip of a blacksmith!"

"Hardly," Marcia laughed. "But they do grow up fast on the frontier."

Suddenly, Cyril bounded in the door.

"Ah. This one looks like a Stanhope! Come shake hands with your uncle, young man."

Cyril's eyes narrowed, and he approached the stranger stiff-legged as a nervous colt. Marcia's eyebrows lifted just a hair, and Cyril remembered his manners. He wiped his hand energetically on his overalls, and then extended it. "Pleased to meet you, sir," he said.

"Pleased to meet you," Uncle Horace replied, shaking Cyril's hand solemnly.

"Cyril, find your brother and get ready for dinner. I was just setting the table," Marcia explained to Millie, "when your Uncle Horace arrived. Would you gentlemen like to sit and talk on the porch?"

"I, for one, would welcome the breeze," Stuart said, leading Uncle Horace away.

Millie's Remarkable Journey

Millie helped her mother finish the dinner preparations while Adah, Zillah, and Fan set the table. *How can Mamma, who has such a merry heart, be so fond of this dour man? And if the father of the Dinsmore family is so grim, what can his children be like?* Millie could feel discouragement begin to rise inside her. *Be strong and courageous*, she reminded herself. *Very strong and courageous.*

When everything was ready, the girls hurried to their rooms to neaten up, but Millie's thoughts continued. *If what I've heard of the lavish hospitality of the South is true, then I'm glad Mamma and Pappa have insisted on manners and kept a formal table at dinnertime. Manners are simply a way of making your guest feel comfortable, Mamma always says. But I can't imagine Uncle Horace being comfortable at all, and certainly not at a casual dinner.*

Millie re-entered the dining room to find Pappa standing behind Mamma's chair to seat her, as always, and Ru waiting behind her own. She glanced around quickly as she took her place. Zillah and Adah were neat and pretty as always; Fan and Annis were clean and tidy; Ru looked so much like Pappa that she had to look twice to ascertain which was which. Don and Cyril . . . where was Cyril? Running footsteps sounded on the stairs. They skidded to a stop just outside the dining room, and Cyril entered calmly. His hair was combed, his face was washed, his shirttail was tucked in, and Ambrosia was draped over his shoulders like a black and white stole. Millie glanced at Uncle Horace. The look on his face would have been comical, if he had not been Mamma's dear uncle. That being the case, it was slightly alarming.

"Cyril!" Stuart's voice was stern. Cyril froze in place, halfway across the room.

"Yes, sir?"

"Gentlemen do not wear skunks to the dinner table. Take Ambrosia outside. We will wait for you."

"Yes, sir." Cyril turned on his heel. "No hats, no skunks. Shirts and shoes . . . ," he was saying to himself as he went out the door, as if to fix the finer points of table etiquette in his brain. When he returned, they all sat down. Stuart prayed, and the meal began. Millie was proud of her younger siblings' manners. She was sure they could dine without shame in the finest restaurant or home. Even little Annis was sweet and polite.

"Millie has to go to the hot place," Annis informed their visitor, "so she'll get better."

"The . . . hot place," Uncle Horace said. "I see. I have heard North Carolina called many things, but I confess, never quite that. I personally think it compares more favorably with heaven. The weather in North Carolina will be good for your sister."

Don passed a bowl of potatoes to his twin as he asked, "How hot is it in North Carolina? Does it ever snow?"

"Occasionally we do get snow and even ice storms in the winter," Uncle Horace said. "But the weather is much warmer than it is here. We have a longer growing season. In the summer, it positively sizzles."

"Gets pretty hot around here in the summer too," Cyril said, in defense of his beloved Indiana.

"In North Carolina," Uncle Horace said seriously, "on a hot summer day, you don't have to bake your potatoes."

"You don't?" Don said. He started to scratch his head, but remembered his manners in time and dropped his hand to his lap.

"No." Uncle Horace put a potato on his plate. "You just pull them from the ground already baked and put on some salt and pepper." Millie raised her napkin to her lips. *Is he making a joke?* His face hadn't changed at all. He looked at Don with the same serious expression he had used when announcing his plans to visit Wealthy. Don was studying his face too, obviously looking for a clue.

"I see," Don finally said, apparently deciding that Uncle Horace at least believed what he had just said.

Cyril leaned back in his chair. Uncle Horace was leading Don on, and Millie could tell that Cyril didn't like it. She could see mischief coming, and toyed with the idea of kicking him under the table, but as he was seated next to their guest, she was afraid her boot would connect with the wrong shin. Cyril glanced sideways at his mother and then picked up his napkin.

"In fact," Uncle Horace said, "last summer it got so hot I saw a mule chain crawl like a snake to get into the shade." Don was looking a little confused, but there was no confusion at all in Cyril.

"Ah-ah-a-hornswaggle!" he exploded into the napkin, and then blew his nose loudly in an attempt to cover up his message to his brother.

"Cyril!" Marcia said. Uncle Horace's eyebrows rose just a hair.

"He is quite right, Marcia. It was 'hornswaggle.' And I should apologize for inciting the incident."

Millie was sure Mamma would have sent Cyril to his room if Ambrosia had not chosen that moment to make her second entrance, this time by way of the window. The skunk managed to knock over a vase of dried flowers on the way, shattering the colored glass and spreading dried flower stalks, petals, and seedpods across the dining room floor. Cyril and Don both leapt to their feet, Cyril calling Ambrosia, and Don starting after her.

"Don, don't step on the glass!" Marcia said.

Cyril scooped the little skunk up in his arms. "It's all right, Ambrosia," he said, soothingly.

Marcia's face was positively red, but Uncle Horace seemed unruffled and unchanged.

"This is an excellent pie, Marcia," he said, offering her the plate. "Won't you have some?"

"Yes, Mamma," Millie said quickly. "Have some pie. I will clean up the vase."

"Son," Stuart said, when Cyril returned from depositing Ambrosia outside once again. "I have been thinking for some time that Mr. Weaver is not coming back for that skunk. You know that God created some creatures to live with man and some to roam free, and skunks, I believe, are meant to be free. I believe it's time that Ambrosia went back to the wild where she belongs."

"But what will I tell Mr. Weaver when he comes back?" Cyril said. His freckles stood out against his white face. "He gave me a whole dollar, Pappa!"

"I'm sorry, son. I will return his dollar, and explain that skunks were not meant to live with boys. Would you like me to take her to the marsh?"

"We'll do it, Pappa," Cyril said in a choked voice. "Me and Don. We'll take her tomorrow."

"I'll go along," Ru offered. "We'll have to go some distance. I'll borrow Gordon's wagon. Don't worry, Cyril, we'll find her a real nice place."

Cyril didn't say a word. Don just looked miserable and smashed his peas with his spoon.

Early the next morning, Ru and the boys set out with Ambrosia riding in Cyril's arms. They were gone until mid-afternoon, and returned without their skunk or their smiles.

43

Millie's Remarkable Journey

At dinner that night, Stuart thanked the Lord for providing food for his family. Millie had already opened her eyes when she noticed that Cyril's head was still bowed, his hands clasped so hard his knuckles were white.

"And dear Lord God," he prayed earnestly, "give Ambrosia her supper. Find her a nice crawdad, or an old duck egg or somethin'. And God, please don't let her be the supper for any other critter—no matter how hard it is prayin' for a meal."

"Amen," Stuart said solemnly.

The rest of the meal was very quiet, even though Uncle Horace tried to liven the talk with news of Roselands and the family there.

The next few days were a whirlwind of preparations and goodbyes for Millie. On the day of her departure, even Cyril was trying to shake off his grief. "I'll help you pack, Millie?" he offered.

"Why, that's thoughtful of you, Cyril," Millie said. "But it won't be hard. Every outfit I own will fit in one trunk, with plenty of room left over for my slippers, boots, and a few books."

"Yeah," Cyril said, rapping his knuckles against it. "That's a big ol' trunk all right. Well, if you need help, let me know." He watched her fold her dresses and lay her petticoats out on her bed. He kept shifting from foot to foot, as if he couldn't think of just the right words to say. Then he sauntered off with his hands in his pockets. Millie shook her head. *Poor Cyril. He really does miss Ambrosia.*

Traveling Light

Millie smoothed a wrinkle from a burgundy skirt, and then folded it carefully. It would be tossed and tumbled as the trunk was moved, of course, but she wanted it folded neatly for at least the first few miles. She packed her slippers and boots at the bottom of the trunk, then her petticoats and pantalets, and finally, she carefully laid her dresses and bonnets in, putting her best dress, the green and black silk one, on top. When she had sewn those seams, she'd had no thought of wearing it anywhere but in Pleasant Plains. It was good to know that she had something of quality and style to wear when she presented herself at Roselands. She shut the lid of the trunk. Everything fit with room to spare, just as she thought it would. Her Bible, sketchbook, and the book she was reading, she placed in her carpetbag, which she would carry with her in the stagecoach. She looked up to find her mother watching, her hand pressed to her mouth.

"What's the matter, Mamma?" Millie asked in alarm.

"Nothing," but there were tears in her mother's voice. "It's just that . . . you look so grown up." Millie went to her quickly, put her arms around her neck, and gave her a kiss.

"Gordon will be by any minute to take your trunk," Marcia said. "And I have just a moment away from the children. Will you come with me, Millie?"

Millie followed her Mamma down the hall to her parents' room.

"I still have a few things left from the old days," Marcia said, opening her jewelry box.

When Millie was a little girl, she used to play with the baubles in that jewelry box as her Mamma prepared to go to the theater or a concert with her Pappa. There had been more jewelry in it then—gold and diamonds, Millie was sure—but that was before her parents lost all their money and moved the family to Pleasant Plains. One by one the baubles had disappeared, as clothing or medicine was needed for one of the children. A fine gold bracelet had disappeared the week before Stuart and Marcia presented the children with a rowboat of their own, and timber to build a pier along the riverbank. When Millie had mentioned it to her Mamma, Marcia had laughed. "I will get more enjoyment from watching my children play than I ever would from wearing that old thing," she had said, and then leaned close to Millie to whisper, "Besides, your Pappa promised to take me rowing in the moonlight!"

Marcia selected a carved ivory bracelet, matching hair combs, and a delicate cameo. "These are suitable for a young woman of your age, I believe," she said. "And if you should happen to attend a Christmas ball . . . "

"I'll wear them for you, Mamma," Millie said.

"Maaaaamaa!" Don bellowed from somewhere down the hall. "Fan can't find her shoes!"

Marcia sighed and then kissed Millie's head. "Let me go get the children ready. They all want to go along to see you off on the stage. Are you all packed?"

"Yes, Mamma."

Millie returned to her room. She started to open the trunk and put the jewelry inside, but then thought better of it. The trunk would be riding on top of the stage, and who knew where on the boats or trains. She didn't want to risk something as precious to her as her mother's jewelry being lost or stolen. Taking a small piece of velvet from her top drawer, she wrapped up the jewelry, and then tucked it in her reticule. Millie slipped the lock on her trunk, snapped it shut, dropped the key in her pocket, and then turned to survey her room once more. She had a feeling that she was forgetting something, but could not think of what it was.

Scrape, scrape, scrape. The sound was barely audible — teeth on wood. *Mice. I'll have to tell Mamma about it while the little ones aren't listening, or they'll beg her not to set traps.*

Heavy footsteps thundered up the stairs, and Gordon appeared at her door. "Your mother said that you were ready for me to carry your trunk," he said.

"I'm all ready," Millie said, waving a hand at the trunk. "If you can carry that, I will bring my bag."

"Of course I can," Gordon said with a smile. He took the handle of the trunk and started to swing it to his shoulder. "Oooof," he said. "What are you hauling in here? Bricks?"

"No bricks," Millie said, puzzled. "A few dresses, shoes, a book or two . . . "

"A book or two? Are you sure you didn't pack an entire library? Better let me go down the stairs first. If this thing falls, I wouldn't want you under it." Millie followed him down the stairs and out the door. Gordon gave a mighty heave, and the trunk cleared the side of the wagon and landed with a thud in the bed of the wagon. "Whew," he wiped his brow. "I didn't think I was going to . . . "

Suddenly, the trunk erupted in a thunderous banging.

"Help!" a muffled voice called. "Help! Let us out!" Gordon leapt into the wagon and tugged on the lock.

"Here!" Millie fished the key out of her pocket and tossed it to him.

Gordon leaned over the trunk and a strange look crossed his face. "Better stand back, Millie," he said. "Stand upwind. This isn't going to be pretty."

Millie backed away as Gordon pulled the lid open. Cyril exploded out of the trunk like a jack-in-the-box; Ambrosia was a streak of black and white fur as she disappeared into the hedge, but the smell she left behind had Cyril rubbing his eyes and crying in between bellows.

Gordon picked him up by the shirt collar and, holding him at arm's length, hauled him to the well. "Water won't wash off the smell," he said, "but it will help your eyes." He shoved Cyril under the spigot and pumped vigorously.

"What on earth is this racket . . . Oh, my!" Marcia put her hand over her nose.

"Mamma!" Millie said when Cyril's eyes had been thoroughly flushed with water. "What will I do? My clothes and shoes . . ." Gordon was fishing things out with a long stick. "My bonnet!" Millie said, and started crying.

"Don't cry, Millie," Gordon said, letting the bonnet slide back into the trunk. "I can't stand to see you cry."

But Millie couldn't help it. Her clothes were ruined beyond thought of redemption, re-use, or repair. So much for pride in her handiwork! Everything she owned had been in that trunk. Even the trunk was irretrievable. Not only had the smell completely permeated the wood, but Cyril had carved air holes in the back panel with his pocketknife. The trunk and everything in it had to be burned at the bottom of the garden. Cyril was scrubbed in a bucket of tomato juice, but he still smelled awful.

The decision to delay the trip for two days was not so much made as forced upon them, though Millie was not sure how a two-day delay would help. The disaster was not as complete as it might have been. Cyril had removed her green and black dress and all of her books to make room in the trunk. He had thrown them under the bed. In addition, Millie had the travel outfit she was wearing.

48

"Ambrosia came back because she loved me," Cyril explained. "So I was runnin' away, an takin' her with me. It's the least a fella can do for someone who loves him. And Ambrosia didn't mean no harm. You must admit, it wasn't altogether mannerly the way Gordon dropped that trunk."

"It wasn't exactly mannerly to stow away inside it," Millie pointed out. "What would I have done without my books?"

Millie discussed the possibilities with her mother. Fabric could be purchased of course, but it took days to sew even one dress. She needed several travel dresses at least, for there would not be time on her journey to make more, or have them made in advance. They ended the discussion no closer to a solution than they had begun. Uncle Horace was clearly upset at the delay. His family was expecting him, and he had a schedule to keep. He initially suggested filling another trunk, and was embarrassed—for himself or for the Keiths, Millie could not tell—when it was explained that *all* of Millie's clothes had been in the one trunk.

Millie went to her room, where she could have some quiet. *Lord, what am I going to do without my clothes?* Pictures of Celestia Ann when she had first appeared on their doorstep flashed through Millie's brain. *Will I be reduced to wearing Ru's overalls beneath my worn gardening dress?*

Tap! Millie looked up. *Tap! Tap!* Someone was throwing gravel at her window. She opened the sash and leaned out. Gordon Lightcap smiled up at her.

"Remember when I told you I could fix things?" he asked.

"Yes," Millie said.

"Good!" He bowed.

"Gordon, what do you mean?" she asked.

49

He just waved over his shoulder and walked away. Zillah arrived a moment later to tell Millie that Helen was at the door.

"I heard about your troubles, Millie," Helen said, handing her a parcel. "I know you can't order dresses in time." The parcel contained several petticoats, a handsome shirtwaist, and a hat. Lu was the next to arrive, with two dresses and several pairs of pantalets. She, too, brought a hat. Soon it seemed the whole Young Ladies Bible Study was in Millie's bedroom, mixing and matching odds and ends brought from their closets and bureau drawers. The only consistent theme seemed to be hats.

"Gordon told us to bring them," Claudina explained. "He said you needed clothes, but were awfully upset about losing your hat."

"My new bonnet," Millie explained. "But these are lovely."

The results of the outfits thrown together ranged from the ridiculous—Lu had excellent taste in clothing, but was twice as wide as Millie—to the workable. Damaris, surprisingly, was almost Millie's twin in size and shape. The three dresses she brought, though plain and somber, were declared a good fit, and when the right hat was added, they assumed a certain sense of style.

Shoes, however, were another matter. Lu's were the closest to Millie's size, but Lu's extravagant taste in footwear looked rather odd with Damaris's sensible fashions, and Lu had an unfortunate fondness for heels. "Tip-toe, tip-toe! Glide!" Lu coached as Millie wobbled across the floor. The entire membership of the Bible study was brushing away tears of laughter before Millie managed a "glide" across the smooth floor. Fortunately, Millie still had the sensible pair of shoes she'd had on the day of the skunk disaster. She could wear them as she traveled.

"I do feel sorry for you, Millie," Helen said as they put the last outfit together. "Having to travel in hand-me-downs."

"I don't care if they aren't new," Millie said, not altogether truthfully. "I have never been so thankful for clothes in my life. I will remember each of you as I wear them."

"Well, be sure to wear my shoes if you go to a hat shop," Lu said.

"I don't think Millie will ever need to shop for hats again," Celestia Ann pointed out logically.

"But if she has the urge to purchase a hat in say, Philadelphia, she should remember that periwinkle is a most becoming color on me."

"Lu!" Claudina said.

"I was just making a joke," said Lu, but she had a hopeful twinkle in her big blue eyes.

Rhoda Jane was the last one to leave. "Here," she said, handing Millie a package. "It's not new, but it's only been worn once. In fact, the night I wore it was the first time I thought that perhaps, just perhaps, there was a God who loved me."

Millie opened the brown paper to find an emerald green dress with french lace at the cuffs and throat.

"Do you think such an old dress will be hopelessly out of fashion?" Rhoda Jane asked.

"This dress will always be in fashion," Millie laughed. But as she sat on the bed after her friends had left, Millie's eyes teared. She wiped them quickly as Marcia came into the room.

"It's marvelous to have friends," Marcia said, sitting on the edge of the bed. "We must remember to thank Gordon as well as the young ladies."

"I will, Mamma, but . . . "

"But?"

"I'm going to look like a bag of rags!" Millie wailed.

"Now, now," Marcia said, taking Millie in her arms. "You cannot possibly look like a bag of rags. The clothes are all very nice, even if the sizes are odd."

Millie could only manage a sniffle against her mother's shoulder. Marcia tipped Millie's chin up and looked deep into her eyes.

"What are you looking for, Mamma?"

"I'm looking to see what Jesus sees. He doesn't look at the outside, you know. Just the heart. Nope. No rags in there—no matter what this girl is wearing. Now, let's pack."

CHAPTER

Getting Acquainted

*Gold there is, and rubies in
abundance, but lips that
speak knowledge are
a rare jewel.*

PROVERBS 20:15

Getting Acquainted

*T*he air was crisp as apples and cool as well-chilled cider when Stuart handed Millie up into the stagecoach two days later. Marcia made sure she had a suitable jacket with clean kerchiefs in the pocket, a rug to warm her legs, and a picnic basket by her side. Stuart had presented her with a fine travel kit for writing—a thin oak box that contained a new steel-nibbed pen, ink, and ample paper. The box itself could serve as a desk.

"Now don't forget to write as soon as you arrive," Stuart said, giving Millie a kiss.

"And you," Marcia said, taking her uncle's hand. "How can we ever thank you?"

"Thank me? The privilege is mine," he said, kissing the hand she had offered him. "Millie will be good company for my own daughters, and a welcome distraction for Mrs. Dinsmore over the winter."

Millie's friends from church, including Gordon and Wallace and the entire Young Ladies Bible Study group, were lined up along the road through the center of town. Millie waved from the open window as the coach rattled by, and they shouted and waved back.

"Come back soon, Millie!"

"Get better!"

"We are going to miss you! And don't forget to bring my shoes back!"

Millie was sure by the smile on Celestia Ann's face that she had organized the whole thing.

"It looks as if Pleasant Plains is losing its favorite daughter," Uncle Horace commented.

Millie's Remarkable Journey

"Nonsense," Millie said. "I am sure they would act this way no matter who was leaving."

At that moment, a red rose flew through the window and landed in Millie's lap. She looked up to see Nicholas Ransquate, his hand over his heart and a new hat on his head, lifting a hand in farewell.

"Really?" Uncle Horace said. "Extraordinarily friendly place, Pleasant Plains."

For the first leg of their journey, Millie and her uncle were the only two passengers in the coach. They made small talk about the weather and the countryside as they left the prairie behind and the stage road wound through woods beautiful with the rich tints of October. Finally, everything that could be said about the beauty of the day and the colors of autumn seemed to be exhausted, and Millie was relieved when her uncle rode silently for a time, gazing out the window.

She pulled the sketchbook and charcoal from her bag and pretended to focus on her art. *What do I talk about to an almost perfect stranger, who just happens to be my uncle?* She worked on a quick study of the shape of a tree they were passing. Surprisingly, even with the jolting of the coach, she was pleased with the result and decided to try something a little more challenging. She surreptitiously studied the lines of her uncle's face. *His profile is so much like Cousin Horace's that if it weren't for the gray at his temples, I would expect to hear Cousin Horace's laugh. Let's see . . . His nose is straight,* she touched the charcoal to the paper, *like so . . .* The stage bounced over a rock. Millie looked down at the paper and frowned. The twisted forms of the trees had been more forgiving of the difficulty of sketching while in a moving coach, but the straight, clean line she had attempted had turned into a bill that would have made a heron envious.

"What are you sketching?" Uncle Horace had turned back from the window.

"Nothing, really," said Millie, quickly turning the book over. "Just practicing my technique."

"I am afraid I will be a boring traveling companion for a young lady," Uncle Horace said with a sigh. "We have hardly begun, and I have run out of things to say. I am not conversant on fashions, or drawing, or music, or any of the things a young lady might study, I'm afraid. I have been told that I am dull company, and sometimes grim, but I assure you my bark is worse than my bite." He paused to look out the window at the passing view, then resumed the conversation. "I owe your mother and your Aunt Wealthy a great debt for the care they gave my son and me when Eva died."

"What was she like?" Millie asked, and then blushed. "I mean . . . if it does not cause you pain to . . . "

"Talking about Eva doesn't cause pain," he said, his face softening just a tiny bit.

Have I ever seen him smile? Millie wondered. She couldn't remember.

"I wish I could have known her longer. I wish I knew her still. Eva was . . . a Stanhope. She loved wild adventures, riding, dancing . . . and she was terrible at keeping her house in order. I had to hire two housekeepers just to keep after her. She could not focus on her duties, or remember her position, it seemed. I came into her dressing room one day to find her on her knees tending a cut on the foot of a slave. I told her to remember her station, but she laughed. She just laughed and said, 'If washing feet was not beneath Jesus, how could it be beneath me?' "

"She was a Christian, then?"

"She became religious after we married. It seems to plague the Stanhopes . . . I apologize. I realize your family is religious also. I hope you won't be afraid to speak your mind around me, Millie."

"You should have no worry on my account, Uncle. I fear I am known for speaking my mind. I thought my parents would have warned you," Millie said with a smile.

"You mean the young people who lined the road as we left were cheering your departure, rather than grieving it?"

"It is altogether possible," Millie laughed, deciding suddenly that she liked this uncle. "I have opinions on most everything."

"As a gentleman, I will defend your right to speak them," he said gallantly, and then seemingly without thinking, pressed his hand to his side. "Though the last time I defended a strong-minded lady, I was shot in the ensuing duel."

"A *duel*, Uncle!"

"A trifle. We were in Charleston, so no law was broken. A gentleman can still defend his honor in South Carolina . . . or the honor of a lady."

"Eva?"

"No," a shadow passed over his face. "Eva would never have understood the event, or she would have laughed it off. But Isabel is cut from a different cloth entirely. Her father is a newspaper publisher in Charleston, of the finest old family—the Breandan family. He was running for office, and his political opponent took liberties with the truth about the family's heritage. Isabel begged me to correct him."

"You killed him for insulting a lady's family?" Millie asked in disbelief.

Getting Acquainted

"Hardly." Uncle Horace almost managed a smile. "I am an abysmal shot, my dear. The pistol went off as I lifted it. I believe Judge Crockett now has nine and one-half toes, rather than the standard ten. His aim proved better. I received a burn along my ribs."

"And that was the end of the matter?"

"Certainly not. The end of the matter was that Isabel agreed to marry me. And she has made a very diligent wife."

"Station comin'!" the driver yelled from above. "It's a little rough."

Millie bounced completely into the air as the stage hit a hole, and then landed with a whump on the seat once more. Uncle Horace grasped the window to keep from being thrown about the inside of the coach. Two more bumps, and the coach lurched to a stop. Millie straightened her hat, which had come down over her left eye, and gathered up her carpetbag and picnic basket, both of which had landed on the floor.

"Now, that warn't so bad!" said the driver, jerking the door open. "One hour for grub and stretchin' yer limbs, folks."

Uncle Horace exited the coach and then helped Millie down. They were in the yard of a small farmhouse in a little clearing in the forest. A litter of hound pups came tumbling out of the newly built barn, and a girl ran from the house to shoo them away from the guests and out from under the horses' hooves.

"Come in, come in!" called the farm wife, a plump, bustling young woman with a large smile and a clean white apron, from the door. They followed her into the rough cabin. It was neat and clean inside, the puncheon floor obviously having been swept and a table prepared for the travelers. "Washtub's out back," she said cheerfully, "with everything you might need." "Everything" turned out to be a bar of rough brown soap, a mirror nailed to the wall, and a clean towel. Millie tidied her hair, washed the travel dust from her face and hands, and returned to the house while Uncle Horace took his turn.

When he returned, he pulled out the bench that ran along one side of the table and seated Millie, and then took the place opposite her. The table sported a neat gingham tablecloth and matching napkins, and was loaded with eggs, bread, butter, coffee, three kinds of vegetables, and stewed dried apple pie for dessert.

"Looks mighty good," the stage driver said, seating himself beside Uncle Horace. Millie had to agree. She was starving. She folded her hands and bowed her head for grace. It was a full minute before she realized that no one else was going to pray. She glanced up, and then wished she hadn't. Uncle Horace was watching her solicitously. The farm wife stood behind him, head bowed, waiting reverently, and the stage driver's mouth was hanging open, displaying the bite he had just taken. His eyes too were fixed on Millie.

"Lord," she said, quickly closing her eyes again. "Oh, Lord . . ." *How can it be, when I talk to You incessantly when I'm alone, that I can't force out a simple prayer when strangers are listening? It's so easy in front of my family!* "Dear Lord . . . thank You. Amen," she blurted out.

"Well, that was certainly to the point," Uncle Horace said. "Would you like a slice of bread?"

I sounded like a complete idiot, Millie thought. She was saved from the necessity of making conversation for the next few minutes by the driver, who talked nonstop, often with his mouth full. *What must Uncle Horace think of prayer if he considers religion a plague?* Millie had read of a child whose best friend existed only in his imagination, and yet he spoke to him and about him as if he were real. *Is that the way Uncle Horace views my prayers — as if I'm speaking to a figment of my imagination?*

Uncle Horace certainly didn't seem to be watching her. He was fully occupied in brushing away a spray of crumbs from his sleeve, delivered on the same breath the driver used to praise the "perfect" cornbread.

"The cornbread is delicious, sir," Uncle Horace said, flicking the last crumb away, "but if I could trouble you to avoid terms such as perfect, polite, or pass the peas, it would make the meal more enjoyable for us all." Uncle Horace had a decidedly strained look on his face.

"Sorry 'bout that," the driver said, wiping his mouth on the back of his hand.

I do care what Uncle Horace thinks. But I care more about what God thinks. Millie lifted her chin. She was determined to say a longer prayer at the next meal, no matter who was listening.

After they finished the meal, Uncle Horace suggested a walk around the clearing to stretch their legs. The stage driver, who had finished eating well before Millie and Uncle Horace — possibly due to the fact that he used his fingers as often as his fork, thus enabling him to eat with both hands — was playing with the puppies in the barnyard. The puppies jumped and tumbled over one another vying for his attention.

"Are your pups for sale?" Uncle Horace asked the little girl who was still watching over them.

Millie's Remarkable Journey

"Yup," she said with a gap-toothed smile. "One dollar apiece. They are prime huntin' dogs, too."

Uncle Horace turned to the driver. "If I were to purchase one," he asked him, "could you deliver it to Pleasant Plains on your next trip?"

"Expect so," the driver said.

Uncle Horace studied the puppies. "What is that one like?" He pointed to a small pup with black ears.

"That's the sweetest one of them all," the girl said.

"That won't do," said Uncle Horace with a frown.

Suddenly, a black and tan pup with two white feet caught sight of him and bounded toward him with a baby growl. It managed to trip over its own ears and sprawled in front of him, then bounced to its feet again, wagging a piti-ful stub of a tail.

"What happened to his poor little tail?" Millie asked.

"Bobcat tried to drag him off for supper," the girl shrugged. "Pup wouldn't go."

Uncle Horace wiggled the toe of his boot and the puppy pounced on it, and then started worrying the cuff on his pants with its needle-like teeth. "Enough of that," Uncle Horace said, picking him up and looking him in the eye. The puppy squirmed, grunted, and attempted to kiss his nose. "What do you think, Millie? Would your parents object? I can't help but feel I was partly at fault for Ambrosia's exile."

"I'm sure they would allow it," Millie said.

"I expect this one will be ten percent off," Uncle Horace said, addressing the little girl.

"Now why would you expect that?" she asked in surprise.

"Because ten percent of this pup is clearly missing," Uncle Horace said seriously, indicating the bobbed tail.

"You would not expect me to pay full price for ninety percent of a dog, surely?"

"Mister, what that pup lacks in tail he makes up for in
bounce. I was thinkin' that one ought to go for one dollar
and ten cents, at least."

"One dollar," Uncle Horace said, narrowing his eyes.
"Not a cent more."

The girl tugged on her braid and considered. "You got a
deal," she said at last.

Uncle Horace borrowed Millie's writing supplies to pen
a quick note to Cyril and Don.

"Throw in an extry two bits," the girl said, "an' I'll tie a
red ribbon round his neck when I send him."

"That would suit perfectly," Uncle Horace said, producing the money.

After the arrangements were made they traveled on,
reaching a little town in time to get their supper and a
night's lodging at its tavern, where the fare and accommodations were on a par with those of the farmhouse. This
time when they sat down for supper, Millie was ready. It
was somewhat easier to pray seated at a small table with
only her uncle to hear.

"Dear Lord," she prayed, "I thank You for keeping us
safe as we travel, and for meeting our needs. Thank You for
the continued good weather. I ask that You bless this meal.
Amen." *There! That was better!* She glanced across the table
at Uncle Horace. He was just snapping shut the cover of his
gold watch. Millie bit her lip. *He couldn't have bowed his head
at all if he were fishing the watch out of his pocket to check the time.
Or perhaps he was timing my prayer?* In which case she hoped
he was disappointed, because this one was at least three
sentences longer. Millie was tired of his constant company,

and she knew he must be tired of hers. She had completely run out of things to say at a quarter past four, and felt the need to refill the reservoir of her soul before they continued. So she excused herself directly after dinner and escaped to the solitude of her room. She was already missing her parents more than she could say.

Millie turned to her Bible first, praying and then reading the book of Ephesians until she felt peace settle about her. Mamma always gave her a special Scripture at bedtime. Tonight she would choose her own. She thought a moment and then opened to John 14:16-17. "And I will ask the Father, and he will give you another Counselor to be with you forever—the Spirit of truth. The world cannot accept him, because it neither sees him nor knows him. But you know him, for he lives with you and will be in you." She copied the verse carefully in her diary.

"Dear Heavenly Father," she wrote. "The world cannot see or know the Holy Spirit that You sent to live in me. But I do know Him, and the world can see my actions and hear my voice. Please help my actions to show Your love. Let my words bring glory to Your Son, and help me to listen to Your Holy Spirit as He speaks truth to my heart and mind." Then she prayed for Uncle Horace, his son Horace Jr., and little Elsie, as well as the stage driver, before she settled into her usual prayers for her family and friends. By the time she blew out the candle, Millie was ready for a peaceful sleep.

They acquired two new passengers the next morning—business partners, one portly and sour and inclined to interrupt and complain, the other thin and overly fond of making jokes. His laughter bore an uncanny resemblance to the hee-haw of the little donkey that Beth Roe kept for a pet. Millie tried hard to keep the comparison from her mind, but his large teeth and thin neck made it all but impossible.

"I hope that is not catching," the rotund partner said the first time Millie pulled a handkerchief from her pocket to cover a cough.

"I haven't caught it yet," Uncle Horace assured him, "and I have been in the company of my niece for several days."

Still, the man wedged his huge body as far from Millie as he could and looked uncomfortable each time she had to cough. The thin man proceeded to tell a series of jokes about patent medicine salesmen. He thought them very funny, even if no one else did. Millie was praying for patience within an hour of departing the station.

The roads they passed over that day were mostly corduroy—made of logs and saplings laid side by side—which produced a constant bouncing. Where one had been displaced or rotted away, the travelers would experience a sudden jolt-thud-jolt, as first the front and then the rear wheels passed through the trough. The bouncing not only made conversation difficult, but there was a real hazard of chipped teeth if your mouth happened to be open at the wrong time. Twice Millie was thrown from her seat and only through the greatest contortion avoided landing on the lap of the round businessman. This caused his thin partner to bray without the necessity of first telling a joke, and Millie to redouble her prayers.

At first, the jarring seemed to aggravate Millie's cough, but oddly enough, as the ride went seemingly endlessly on, she began to breathe more easily, as if the constant pounding had somehow helped to clear her lungs.

Millie's Remarkable Journey

They reached Delphi on the Wabash River, sore, weary, and very glad to make the change both of mode of transportation and of company. Millie was numb from her toes to her earlobes from the constant vibration. When she first stepped off the stage, she was sure something was amiss, but soon realized that she had grown so accustomed to the rattling of her teeth that she missed it now that it was gone.

They boarded a boat that carried them down the Wabash and up the Ohio River to Madison, where they landed again and passed part of a day and night. Their trunks were transferred to a larger craft and they continued on their way up the Ohio River. The larger boat gave Millie the luxury of a little more privacy in a tiny room of her own, and the opportunity to talk freely with her uncle for the first time in days.

"And what are you thinking of with such a serious expression?" Uncle Horace asked Millie one afternoon when he found her leaning against the rail, watching a barge loaded with goods slide by on the busy Ohio. She had come on deck with every intention of working on her sketchbook but had been distracted by the river traffic.

"I was thinking that the construction of canals was truly visionary," she said. "Ohio was not a wealthy state until the completion of the Ohio and Erie Canal. Farmers had good soil, but no way to get produce to market in the cities. Do you have many canals in the South?"

"We hardly need them," Uncle Horace said. "Our states are far more rural, with large plantations many miles apart. The equivalent of your small farmer could not eke out a living in the South. Cotton or tobacco require many acres to make a profit, and our soil is not fit for anything else. We are beginning to build a respectable rail system, however."

Getting Acquainted

"It's good that you are improving the railways. I don't believe a country as large as ours can exist long without a sound system of transportation," Millie said. "Every state should work on improving it."

Horace's eyebrow twitched. "Are you parroting your father, or is this opinion your own?"

"My own, Uncle." Millie was growing accustomed to his gruff, abrupt manner. "My father encourages all of his children to read broadly and to think about what we read."

"Now this must be your mother's influence," he said, pointing at her sketchbook. "I am glad that Marcia has seen fit to educate you in the more ladylike arts. May I see your sketches?" Millie tried to think of a polite way to decline, but not finding one, hesitantly handed over the book.

"Hmmm," Uncle Horace said as he flipped through the first few pages. "Ummm." He stopped at the picture of the muskrat. "Well! This one shows promise!"

Millie sighed. "I wish I could take credit for it," she said, explaining about Gordon.

The next picture was the tree Millie had sketched on their stage ride, and she felt justified in the twinge of pride she experienced when he complimented it. He started to turn another page, and Millie realized suddenly what the next drawing was.

"I don't think I would go any further," Millie began, but he had already turned the page, only to be confronted with his own profile—with the addition of a beak for a nose. She held her breath as he turned it this way and that, squinting. "This . . . hillside with precipice . . . is lovely. Did you see it out the window as well?"

Millie teetered between mirth and chagrin, finally falling into laughter. "That is a picture of you, Uncle." She reached over and turned the picture right side up. "The *aristocratic* nose is courtesy of a poorly timed bump in the road."

"I see." He handed the book back. "And are you as accomplished at the piano?"

"Oh, more so I hope," Millie said, still laughing. "I've spent many hours over the last two winters sitting at the piano in church to work on hymns, and not a few playing with Mrs. Lightcap. And I rarely play piano while being tossed about in a stagecoach."

"Probably wise," he said, and Millie was sure he almost smiled. Then he observed, "You must come as something of a shock to the Ladies Society, Millie Keith. Young women may have minds, but they are not encouraged to use them in the realm of politics, commerce, or science. And if I am not mistaken, you are a keen observer and love to learn."

Yes, and more of a shock than you might imagine! thought Millie. Although she had discussed politics and religion with her uncle openly, she had been unable to broach the subject of slavery. Every time it had come up, her tongue had seemed to stick to the roof of her mouth. But she *had* been watching carefully, learning what she could. As they traveled east, she saw that the passengers around them became more varied, both in fashion and in lifestyle. Millie brushed shoulders with the poor and the rich, with working class people and with aristocracy. She observed free blacks traveling on business, as well as one or two slaves, although she was never able to speak to any of them, since it was quite improper for a young lady to strike up an acquaintance without an introduction, and she had no intention of embarrassing her uncle. There was something in her uncle's manner toward both the slaves and the free blacks that made her uncomfortable, but she was unable to pinpoint exactly what.

On the large steamboat there were many more personal slaves traveling with their masters. They seemed diligent and caring, as her cousin Horace Jr.'s slave, John, had been. They did act as servants, and Millie had tended enough sick, washed enough linen, and cooked enough meals for the poor to know that there was no shame in serving others. Jesus came as a servant, after all. *Could Helen have been right about the abolitionist papers? Have I been believing lies?*

CHAPTER

A Brief Visit

*"Let me get you something
to eat, so you can be
refreshed and then
go on your way."*

GENESIS 18:5

A Brief Visit

*T*he boat carried them as far as Portsmouth where they boarded yet another stage to cross the countryside to Lansdale. Millie was relieved that the roads of Ohio were so much more developed; the stage ride was almost smooth. Suddenly she noticed the shapes of the hills becoming familiar—like something from a dream—and then the steeple of a church rose over the tree-tops. The bushes parted like a theater curtain on each side of the road, and they were rattling over the cobblestone streets of Lansdale.

Here the coach moved more slowly, as the streets were full of bustling pedestrians, mule carts, drays, and people on horseback. Millie scanned the sidewalks eagerly, look-ing for familiar faces. Her stay in Lansdale would be so short that she had no hope of seeing all her friends, but she did hope that Aunt Wealthy had sent notes to Annabeth, Camilla, and Bea when she received Mamma's letter. It would be horrible to pass through without seeing them.

Millie saw a few familiar faces on the street, but many more strangers, as well as storefronts and homes being built. Lansdale was growing and prospering. Several of the women were wearing bustles, a fashion Millie had read about but never seen, consisting of a pad or frame that puffed out the back of their skirts. The stagecoach stopped at a crossroads to let a farm wagon pass, and Millie watched in fascination as two well-bustled women walked down the street, the padding swaying gently—like the waddle of a duck.

73

Millie's Remarkable Journey

Millie thought of the tooth-jarring corduroy roads she had traveled only days before. If sitting on a bustle was anything like sitting on a pillow, it might be worth the trouble and expense. It could make the three-hour stay on a hard church pew much more agreeable, too. More than once Millie had left church with certain portions cold and numb.

"A penny for your thoughts?" asked Uncle Horace.

Millie jumped. *Of all the times for Uncle Horace to ask!* "I was thinking of . . . ," she pinked slightly, "ladies' fashions."

"Ah! You and Isabel will have something in common after all!" Uncle Horace said, relief evident in his voice.

The stage drew up outside Aunt Wealthy's house. Uncle Horace stepped out and then handed Millie down. "You go ahead," he said. "I'll bring the bags."

Millie ran to the iron gate and swung it wide. The front of the house was just as she remembered it. How she had longed for this house and this town when she had first arrived in Pleasant Plains! Millie smiled. Lansdale was still dear to her heart, but it didn't feel like home. Home was the frontier.

The door opened before Millie could rap on the knocker and Aunt Wealthy stood before her. Aunt Wealthy's warm red coat was buttoned up, and her parasol was over her arm; she was obviously setting out on a walk. Surprise registered briefly on her face, and then her arms were around Millie's neck and they were both weeping. Wannago, Wealthy's little dog, wiggled out of the front of the coat where he had been riding and danced in mad circles around them both, leaping and yapping for joy.

"Dear child!" Aunt Wealthy said, as Millie scooped Wannago into her arms and buried her face in his fur. "This is a delightful surprise! But where are the rest?"

"Here," said Uncle Horace, who had just come up the walk with his valise and Millie's carpetbag. "Haven't you a word of welcome for me?"

Aunt Wealthy's hand flew to her heart and she gasped. "Horace Dinsmore! I have never been more deprised or surlighted! I mean despised and indicted! Er, surmised and invited . . . oh, heavens!"

"Surprised and delighted?" Uncle Horace offered.

"That's it exactly!" Aunt Wealthy said. Millie was sure she was surprised, but wondered if delighted was quite the word to convey the expression on Aunt Wealthy's face. While she had been quite pink with joy seconds before, she was ghostly pale now.

"Aunty, are you feeling well?" Millie asked with concern.

"Of course I am well!" Aunt Wealthy said. "Never been more well! I wasn't expecting anyone, that's all. I was just on my way out." She pulled the door shut behind her.

"Aren't you going to invite us in?" Uncle Horace said.

"In? Into my house?" she asked, somewhat alarmed.

"That was the general idea," Uncle Horace said, frowning slightly.

"This trunk is getting heavy," said the coachman, who had followed Uncle Horace up the path.

"You *did* get Mamma's letter, didn't you, Aunty?" Millie asked.

"I'm afraid not," Aunt Wealthy said.

"Oh, I see," said Uncle Horace, shaking his head. "I'm sure we can find accommodations at the nearest hotel."

"Nonsense!" Wealthy said, seeming to recover herself. She turned and grasped the door handle, pushed it open, and looked in, glancing around the empty room as if she had expected it to have filled with burglars in her short absence. When the burglars failed to make an appearance, she pushed the door completely open. "Come in, come in, all of you. You must be cold, tired, and hungry. I hope you've come to make a long stay!"

The coachman followed them inside, depositing Millie's trunk and going back for Uncle Horace's.

Aunt Wealthy was surreptitiously glancing behind chairs and couches. When Uncle Horace turned to pay the coachman for his trouble, she pulled the curtains aside, snatched a doily from the windowsill, and stuck it in her coat pocket.

"Shall I carry these upstairs?" the coachman asked.

"No!" Aunt Wealthy said quickly. "I mean not yet. We'll carry them ourselves, thank you. Let me ask the maid to prepare the rooms first." She ushered the coachman out and shut the door behind him, and then turned to Millie and Uncle Horace. "Sit right here in the parlor while I take care of everything. I'd better tell the cook to set two more places for dinner tonight. I'll be right back."

A maid and a cook? Millie shook her head as she sat down to scratch Wannago's ears. She had never known Aunt Wealthy to employ servants. She certainly hadn't mentioned anything about them in her letters. Wealthy Stanhope not only loved preparing exotic foods, but her recipes extended to fireproofing laundry and medicinal rubs and remedies for many common ailments. She was so fond of experimenting in the kitchen that the Keith children had all learned to ask what it was before they tasted a tempting concoction bubbling on her stovetop. Millie could not imagine her aunt employing a servant to cook for just one person. *Could she be having health problems she hasn't told us about?* Visions of Mrs. Lightcap filled Millie's brain, and she bit her lip.

A Brief Visit

"Does Aunt Wealthy seem a little . . . strange to you?" Millie asked, as voices drifted from the back of the house.

"I have never known a day when Wealthy Stanhope wasn't strange," Uncle Horace said, removing his coat. "Wealthy is a true original." There was a loud thumping and bumping and scraping upstairs. "Perhaps they are chasing out tigers," he said.

"There!" Aunt Wealthy said, entering the room minus her red coat and parasol, and looking much happier all around. "Everything is taken care of! How you have grown, Millie! And you couldn't be more welcome than you are, brother, though you would have fared a little better provender-wise if I had received word that you were coming." She seated herself on the couch beside Millie.

"I'm sure Mamma wrote," Millie said. "The letter should have preceded us."

"Well, we won't fret about it," Aunt Wealthy responded cheerily. "I am too happy to see you to fret about anything at all! Millie, you are so thin! Your mother has written me about your health, and I have kept you in my prayers. You have come to stay the winter with me and have a good rest, haven't you?"

Millie wished suddenly that she could stay with Aunt Wealthy, to make sure her aunt was really all right and to care for her if need be.

"No, no. She belongs to me for the winter," Uncle Horace said before Millie could open her mouth. "If you want her company, sister Wealthy, you must make up your mind to be our guest also. What is to hinder you from shutting up your house and going with us to Roselands? I am sure I need not say that we would be delighted to have you do so."

"You are very kind, brother," she said, giving him an affectionate look. "But there are reasons why it would not do for me to leave home for so long a visit. Where is Horace Jr., my dear sister Eva's son? I wish he had come with you, poor boy," she sighed.

The faint frown that had lingered on Uncle Horace's brow since their arrival was now gathered into a storm of wrinkles. He stood and began pacing, as if his unsettled thoughts would not leave his body in peace. "He is hardly the subject for pity," he said. "Horace Jr. is in Europe with pleasant prospects before him and in apparently excellent spirits."

"Ah, yes," Aunt Wealthy said. "I knew he had gone. He has his child with him, I hope?"

"His child?" Uncle Horace glanced at Millie. "Certainly not. What could he do with her? I had hoped that you knew nothing about that ridiculous affair. Pray how did you learn of it?"

"Horace wrote to me of it himself," Aunt Wealthy said, "after confiding to Marcia and Millie."

"Millie!" he looked even more annoyed. "What was the boy thinking?"

"That they would understand his hurting heart, I imagine. Is little Elsie still with her guardian?"

"Yes, and will be for years to come, I trust. It's no wonder that you were shocked to see me, Wealthy. I had hoped that you would never learn of how Horace had sullied the Dinsmore name and brought shame to his mother's family as well. I apologize on behalf of my son, since he hasn't the sense to do it himself. His mad escapade — I can call his hasty, ill-timed, imprudent marriage by no other name — has been to me a source of untold mortification and annoyance."

A Brief Visit

"Apologize!" said Aunt Wealthy. "I hardly think that is necessary! It was not a bad match, I understand, except for their extreme youth."

"It was most decidedly so!" Uncle Horace exclaimed. "Elsie Grayson was very rich, but she had no breeding. Her father made all of his money by trade. By trade! She was not a fit match for my son, and I consider it a fortunate thing that she did not live."

Millie sucked in her breath at the hardness of his face, and the cruelty of his words. This was a side of Uncle Horace that she hadn't seen, and it frightened her.

"It would have been, in my estimation," he continued, each word so sharp it cut the air, "still more fortunate if her child had died with her."

"Horace Dinsmore, you prideful prig!" Aunt Wealthy said, rising to her full five feet and looking him in the eye. "She is your lawful grandchild, and a poor, motherless babe, too! You may think it quite acceptable to speak of her in this way, but may I remind you that she is also my grandniece? I do not find it acceptable, and I am perfectly willing to extend every benefit of my family affection to her—including standing up to you, sir! Your own grandchild. For shame, Horace!"

"Old Grayson's grandchild," he muttered, turning away. "Please do not mention this subject again, either of you."

"Don't be ridiculous! Of course I will speak up for little Elsie whenever and wherever I can!" Aunt Wealthy said.

Uncle Horace made an unintelligible noise and grabbed his hat. "I'm going out for a look at your town," he said, but turned back at the door. "Wealthy Stanhope, you are the most exasperating of women!"

"And your most affectionate sister-in-law," Aunt Wealthy said firmly as he shut the door.

Millie's Remarkable Journey

Millie could only shake her head. *How could I possibly have thought Aunt Wealthy was becoming feeble-minded?* "You amaze me, Aunty," Millie said when she had recovered her breath enough to speak. "Have you always invoked such thundering?"

Aunt Wealthy nodded. "Always, I'm afraid. Horace has a hot temper and I manage to bring it out somehow. But he does have a good heart. I wish he would listen to it more often. He is disgruntled, but never fear, he will come back in that door within the hour, as calm and in control as he can be. Will you be here long enough to renew old acquaintances, Millie?"

"We leave tomorrow, Aunty. But I just couldn't bear the thought of passing Lansdale without having at least a short visit with you."

"And how is your family?" Aunt Wealthy asked.

Millie proceeded to share news of the family for the next half hour. Aunt Wealthy was wiping tears of laughter from her eyes over the account of Cyril and the skunk-in-a-trunk when Uncle Horace returned, disgruntled no more. In fact, he acted as if nothing had happened.

"If you could stay an extra day, brother," Wealthy offered, "I believe we could do some profitable shopping. Millie must be woefully short of wardrobe."

"I'm afraid we are on a tight schedule," he said. "My wife is expecting me, and we want to return home before the cold weather sets in. We have already had one delay. But don't worry, Wealthy. I won't allow Millie to be dressed like an orphan. I plan to let Isabel take Millie to her own couturier in Philadelphia, where we will purchase the best of everything. I do take responsibility for Ambrosia being in the trunk, after all."

"Are you starving?" Aunt Wealthy said, abruptly changing the subject. "Let me check on the meal." She returned after a few moments to say that dinner was prepared. "It won't be formal, I'm afraid. I had promised the servants the evening off. We will serve ourselves and pretend it's a picnic."

"That is just as well," Horace confessed as they followed Aunt Wealthy into the dining room. "I must admit I have never been comfortable with white servants. It seems so unnatural. I always have the urge to offer them my seat and take their place."

"I confess I always have the same impulse when I am served." Aunt Wealthy smiled up at him as he pulled out her chair and seated her.

Millie blinked. *Could Aunt Wealthy really be agreeing with Uncle Horace? But then, what she said was not an agreement about slavery. Or was it?* She opened her mouth to ask for a clarification, but before her first word could be spoken, Aunt Wealthy interrupted. "Let's thank the Lord for what He has given us." Millie bowed her head, terribly relieved to have someone else pray over the meal.

"Dear Lord," Wealthy began, "Thank You for bringing Millie and Horace here today, and I invite You to be here with us during this meal and during this visit. 'Let the sea resound, and everything in it, the world, and all who live in it. Let the rivers clap their hands, let the mountains sing together for joy; let them sing before the Lord, for he comes to judge the earth.' "

Nobody prayed like Aunt Wealthy. She had been memorizing Scripture for so many years that it often spilled out of her, mixing with her own sincere words and thoughts. Millie loved the sound of it, the joy in her aunt's voice. She couldn't resist peeking through her lashes at Uncle Horace. His eyes were shut and his head bowed reverently. She felt a sudden urge to kick his shin under the table, but closed her eyes quickly instead.

"He will judge the world in righteousness and the peoples with equity," Aunt Wealthy continued. "He provides the berries for our pies and the family to share them with. His love endures forever! Amen."

Aunt Wealthy looked up with a twinkle in her eye. "I love to think about God in the very beginning—creating blackberry bushes, bees for honey, wheat, and salt for crust, all of which are very good by themselves, of course. But don't you think He had pies in mind, even in the first days of creation?" Aunt Wealthy was obviously referring to the still bubbling-hot blackberry pastry on the sideboard.

"And cows!" Millie added. "And sweet butter for the crust, too!"

"That's right. How could I forget cows? I think He created all the ingredients like a glorious puzzle, and then just sat back, waiting for us to put them together. He made the parts and we make the pies. I don't suppose we are ever going to run out of new things to discover."

Millie realized that Uncle Horace was not joining in the conversation. He sat with a polite expression frozen on his face. Aunt Wealthy apparently noticed the same thing. "Millie has told me all about the family in Pleasant Plains, Horace," Aunt Wealthy said, turning to him. "Now, tell me about your trip."

Uncle Horace described the journey, and then went on to tell of the doings of his own family. Conversation continued in this vein throughout the meal.

"Now, if you will direct me to my room, I will leave you ladies to catch up," Horace said. "I am weary."

"Of course," said Aunt Wealthy. She led him up the stairs.

Millie cleared the table, setting the dishes on the sideboard while the water heated on the stove. *If Aunt Wealthy has given the servants the night off, then these dishes have to be done, and I've certainly washed enough dishes to know how.*

"I didn't know you employed servants," Millie said when her aunt returned. "I never remember your keeping them before."

"There are a few things about me that you do not know," Aunt Wealthy said with a smile. "I have had over half a century in which to store up surprises, after all. You leave those dishes where they are, Millie Keith, and come upstairs."

"But . . ."

"No buts," said Aunt Wealthy. She took Millie's hand and led her up the stairs to a guest room.

Millie's trunk was at the foot of the bed and her nightclothes were laid out. *The servants must have carried it up while we ate or before they left for the evening*, thought Millie.

Aunt Wealthy closed the door and leaned against it, and suddenly her whole manner changed. "Millie," she said, and then paused, as if she were searching for the right words. "Have you discussed your abolitionist views with your Uncle Horace?"

"No. Why?" replied Millie, sinking onto her bed. "Surely it wouldn't cause trouble. It seems to me that your sister Eva must have had abolitionist leanings. I believe Uncle Horace loved her very much."

"He did," Aunt Wealthy agreed. "But that was almost twenty years ago and things have changed. Do you still read the *Liberator*?"

Millie's Remarkable Journey

"I thought it had ceased publication," Millie said. "We stopped receiving copies last spring. In fact, we haven't heard much about abolition at all in the past few months."

"William Lloyd Garrison has never missed an issue," Aunt Wealthy said. "They are being stolen from mail bags and destroyed."

"Why, Aunty?"

Aunt Wealthy shook her head. "I have worked against slavery all my life, written letters and pushed for political action. In the last few years, I have seen a sea-change, as Shakespeare would say. Twenty years ago, when my sister married Horace, many people in the southern states would have agreed that slavery was wrong, even evil. They believed—we all did, it seemed—that since the slave trade from Africa had been made illegal, slavery would die out and a new system would take its place. We were wrong."

"Certainly, if people knew that it was evil . . . "

"The slave holders of the South were faced with a choice," Aunt Wealthy said. "They could change their way of life, or they could change the way they thought about slavery. Greed has won out over right thinking, I'm afraid."

"Greed?"

Aunt Wealthy sat down on the edge of the bed beside Millie. "Greed and pride. You see, the wealth of the plantation owners is not in their land or their cotton. It is in human flesh. Their slaves are worth more than their land and their homes combined. If they were to free their slaves, families accustomed to great wealth and power would be left penniless. The price of obeying God would be instant poverty. And that is a price most refuse to pay. So they must convince themselves that slavery is right, that they are not sinning."

Millie took her aunt's hand. "Mamma and Pappa had hoped things were changing for the better. In the last issue of the *Liberator* we received, Garrison wrote that black children born on our soil are American citizens and entitled to all the rights and privileges of any other citizen. Of course that is true. Mamma and Pappa hoped that people were listening."

"I pray to God that He hastens the time when those children will be treated as citizens, but it seems further away today than ever before," Aunt Wealthy said. "The *Liberator* and papers like it are having an effect. The more people hear about the inhumanity of slavery, the more they are forced to think and to take a stand. The southern slave owners are afraid, Millie, afraid of abolitionist ideas, because if enough people believe those ideas, their way of life is doomed. People who are afraid do terrible things. Garrison is a courageous man. And if he traveled to the South today, he would be killed. You must be very careful, Millie."

"Surely you are not saying that Uncle Horace . . . "

"Of course not. I believe you can trust your uncle to protect you in any circumstance and to honor your parents' wishes. But I have not met the new Mrs. Dinsmore. It may be well to keep your own counsel until you see how things stand with her."

"I will be careful, Aunty. I know my parents prayed very hard over whether or not to send me, and I know God can keep me wherever I go. It will only be for the winter."

"But?" said Aunt Wealthy, sensing there was more.

"It has only been a few days, and I am homesick already," Millie confessed. "I am so used to praying with Mamma and Pappa, and talking to them about the Lord. I feel like such a baby."

Millie's Remarkable Journey

"I know exactly how you feel," Aunt Wealthy said.

"You do? But you're . . ."

"Older than dirt?" said Aunt Wealthy. "That's true, and I still sometimes feel very alone, and even afraid. I know it's hard to believe, but sometimes I feel very small. Tiny, in fact, with the whole world against me. Then I remember who God is, and who I am. Look." She picked up a Bible that was lying on the table and turned to Isaiah 43. "This verse has comforted me in my very hardest times. 'But now, this is what the Lord says—he who created you, O Wealthy, he who formed you, Miss Stanhope: "Fear not, for I have redeemed you; I have summoned you by name; you are mine." ' "

"Are you sure that's what it says?" Millie was laughing now. "I was certain that verse read 'He who created you, O Jacob.' "

"Quite sure," Aunt Wealthy said seriously. "But God wrote the Bible for me, you know. And for you, too. You can put your name in many verses. 'For God so loved Millie Keith that he gave his one and only son, that if Millie believes in him, she shall not perish, but have eternal life,' for instance. It comforts me to know I am that dear to Him. I love this whole passage of Isaiah. Listen to this. 'Since you are precious and honored in my sight, Wealthy Stanhope, and because I love you, I will give men in exchange for you, and people in exchange for your life. Do not be afraid, for I am with you . . . .' " She closed the Bible and continued to recite, line and verse, to the end of the chapter. "I memorized that one. The times I have needed it, I have been all alone and often in the dark—times when I needed my Savior to rescue me. You will be no further from Jesus at Roselands than you would be in Pleasant Plains by your mother's side, Millie. I would ask you to stay with me, but I fear your lungs are not strong enough for an Ohio winter."

"Mamma and Pappa promised to pray for me every day," Millie said.

"And I will, too," Aunt Wealthy said.

They talked on into the night, until Aunt Wealthy's eyes were drooping and she could barely hide her yawns. "You need your sleep," she said at last. "We will still have half of tomorrow to talk." She kissed Millie's head before saying goodnight.

Millie listened as her aunt's steps went down the hall to her own room. Millie lay in the darkness for a few moments, trying to sort her thoughts and the information Aunt Wealthy had given her. She prayed for a time, and then pulled the down comforter up to her chin and closed her eyes. Sleep refused to come. In the back of her mind, something tickled. It felt exactly as if she had left her chores undone. *The dishes! Aunt Wealthy went to her room, not downstairs to the kitchen.* Years of habit were too strong to deny. Millie could not sleep a wink with dirty dishes on the sideboard. She rose and lit a candle, and then crept down the stairs, stubbing her toe at the bottom. She was glad that Aunt Wealthy and Uncle Horace were sleeping too far away to hear her cry out. She was more careful as she hobbled down the hall to the kitchen.

There was a light under the door. *Who is awake?* Millie wondered. "Hello?" she called softly as she pushed the door open. The kitchen was empty, but the atmosphere in the room felt somehow unsettled, as if someone had just left. "Hello?" Millie called a little louder. "Uncle Horace? Aunt Wealthy?"

The dishes on the sideboard were gone—not only washed, but dried and put away. There were two plates on the kitchen table—one with a half-eaten piece of blackberry pie on it, the other empty. There was no silverware on the table, but a rag doll leaned against the tea cozy, looking solemnly at the empty plate.

"Millie, what on earth are you doing?"

Millie jumped at the sound of Aunt Wealthy's voice. "I came back down to do the dishes and found a mystery," Millie said. "Is this your pie, Aunty?"

"Blackberry is my favorite," Aunt Wealthy said. She looked around the table, apparently forgetting that she had no fork, and then scooped up a piece of pie with her fingers. "Won't you have some?"

"No, thank you," Millie said, but her voice was choked. "Are you . . . all right, Aunty?"

Aunt Wealthy sighed and looked her in the eye. "You know I would never lie to you, don't you?"

"Of course not!"

"Good. Then let's just go back to bed, dear. And we won't talk about it any more."

Millie looked from the pie to the doll and finally to her aunt, who was licking the last bit of blackberry from her finger. "All right," said Millie.

Aunt Wealthy led her to the kitchen door and then, taking Millie's arm, she said, "We won't talk about it to *anyone.*"

Millie nodded, and they went upstairs together. Aunt Wealthy led Millie to her room, kissed her cheek, and said, "Now stay in bed, dear."

Pictures flashed through Millie's mind: Aunt Wealthy wandering the house, hair in disarray, clutching a rag doll. Eating pie with her fingers and talking to herself. *Is Aunt Wealthy losing her mind? Is she going to wander the streets of Lansdale, talking to poles like Mrs. Lightcap did? Lord, don't let*

A Brief Visit

that happen! Mrs. Lightcap has her children to look after her, but Aunt Wealthy has no one at all! She's all alone in Lansdale! A tear trickled down Millie's cheek. *How can I help her, Lord? I can write Mamma, but she won't be able to leave the children and come. Perhaps I should stay myself. Help me know what to do, Lord Jesus.*

Millie fell asleep praying, but she was just as unsure the next morning when Aunt Wealthy greeted her cheerfully, as if nothing had been amiss the night before.

"Are you feeling better this morning?" Millie asked.

"Better than what?" Aunt Wealthy asked in wide-eyed surprise. "I haven't been this healthy in years, my dear."

Millie watched her carefully all morning, but Aunt Wealthy seemed to be her usual, cheerful self. *Just like Mrs. Lightcap did after a bad spell.* The thought brought tears to Millie's eyes again.

The October weather had turned cold and the air stabbed like ice needles at Millie's lungs, bringing on one coughing fit after another. Aunt Wealthy insisted they stay at home by the fire rather than walking through town, and she served them hot chocolate and buttered biscuits which she made herself. The servants had apparently made it a long holiday, not returning from their night out, but Aunt Wealthy didn't seem to feel this was odd at all. *She's not only ill, she's ill-used by her servants,* Millie thought. *I wish she had stayed with us in Pleasant Plains!*

The talk around the fire, while pleasant, was not intimate, on account of Uncle Horace being present. Just before ten o'clock, there came a knock at the door and Millie opened it to find Annabeth, Beatrice, and Camilla.

"Did you think for one instant that you could pass through Lansdale without seeing your best friends?" Bea asked.

Millie's Remarkable Journey

"I wanted to see you three so much!" Millie cried, pulling them inside. "But when I learned that the letter to Aunt Wealthy did not arrive, I gave up hope. How did you find out I was in town?"

"I selfishly kept you all to myself last night," Aunt Wealthy said. "But I sent round a note this morning. We will leave you young ones to your talk," Aunt Wealthy said, looking significantly at Uncle Horace. "I'm sure you girls have much to catch up on."

There was an awkward moment after Millie's aunt and uncle left the room, and then everyone was hugging and talking at once. Millie soon discovered that Camilla still squeaked when she giggled. Annabeth was taller, quite an elegant young lady. Bea was a little rounder than she had been, and just as merry. Camilla was no longer attending school, having finished the highest grade offered by Mr. Martin. She was continuing with private tutoring, and hoped to travel to a girl's school in London. Annabeth, sweet and quiet as always, sat and watched her friends talk, exchanging smiles with Millie.

"My goodness!" Bea exclaimed, examining Millie's outfit. "Fashions are backward in Indiana. I knew they would be."

"Bea!" Camilla said. "What a thing to say! I'm sure Millie didn't travel all this way to hear your view of frontier fashions."

"Oh! Oh dear!" Bea turned pink. "I didn't mean . . . "

"Never mind," Millie said, giving her red-faced friend a hug. "I know I look like an odd duck." She explained about Cyril's pet, and then gave all of the news of the family. "And what has been happening here?" she asked at last. "Surely there has been some excitement not covered in your letters."

Bea and Camilla both looked to Annabeth, who dropped her eyes.

"What is it?" Millie cried, going to her friend. "Annabeth? What is your news?"

Annabeth held up her left hand to show a simple but elegant ring.

"You are engaged to be married?" Millie was clearly stunned.

"I didn't know how to tell you, Millie. I know that you and Frank were . . . "

"Frank Osborne was my very good friend," Millie said, taking her hand. "That is all. I am delighted. But *married*, Annabeth! It seems so strange."

"Not so strange. I will be eighteen, after all."

"That's right," Millie said, sitting down. "I still have you all fixed in my mind at twelve and thirteen, the way you were when I left. How odd that you have all grown up."

"And you, of course, are still twelve, are you not?" Camilla laughed.

"Speaking of growing old," Millie said, lowering her voice. "Have you noticed any . . . change in Aunt Wealthy?"

"Change?" Bea said. "She practically runs the town. The fabric stores could not survive without her, the charities would be destitute, and the church would simply have to shut its doors."

"I have been worried." Millie couldn't force herself to frame the words. "Will you visit her now and then?"

"If she will let us in," Camilla said. "She is sometimes . . . "

At that moment Aunt Wealthy herself stepped into the room to tell Millie the stagecoach was at the door and it was time for Millie to leave.

Millie's Remarkable Journey

The trunks and bags were loaded. Millie hugged all of her friends at least three times each and tried again to persuade Aunt Wealthy to accompany her to Roselands. Aunt Wealthy assured her there was urgent business at hand that she could not leave. Finally, the driver called and Millie could delay no longer. She wrapped her shawl around her shoulders and prepared to go.

"Don't you have a heavy coat?" Annabeth asked. "It's cold out here!"

"I am afraid it was spoiled by the skunk. The weather was still quite mild when we left Pleasant Plains, and in the rush no one remembered a coat. I'm sure Mamma would have given me her own."

"Pish-tosh," Aunt Wealthy said. "That can soon be remedied." She took her red wool coat from the coat tree by the door and handed it to Millie.

"I can't take yours!" Millie protested.

"Of course you can. I will get another today. Now put it on." Millie put it on. It was rather short in the tail and sleeves, but fit well otherwise. "It's fortunate that I buy my coats too big so that Wannago can wear them with me," Aunt Wealthy said, "or it would never do. And here!" She handed Millie a jar of ointment. "I modified Dr. Cook's recipe for Healing Balm this morning before you woke. Rub this on your chest at bedtime. It will help with your cough. It's also excellent for cuts, burns, and gout, I believe."

Millie kissed her aunt, hugged her friends one last time, and boarded the stage. She had to fight an impulse to jump out, run back, and wrap her tiny aunt in her arms. Uncle Horace said his goodbyes as well, and the driver's whip cracked. Millie thought her heart would break as she watched Aunt Wealthy, standing coatless and shivering in the road, waving goodbye. She looked so alone, even standing in front of Annabeth, Bea, and Camilla. *How could they not have noticed her odd behavior?*

"This is what the Lord says," Millie whispered, "he who created you, O Wealthy, he who formed you, Miss Stanhope. Fear not, for I have redeemed you; I have summoned you by name; you are mine." *Please, please, take care of her, Jesus!*

CHAPTER

6

Wounded Pride

But you — who are you to judge your neighbor?

JAMES 4:12

Wounded Pride

*M*illie wouldn't have missed staying up half the night with Aunt Wealthy for the world, but it left her uncommonly tired the next day. She leaned her arms on the open window of the coach and rested her head on them. Uncle Horace had found a travel companion of like age and interests. They were discussing politics and seemed in agreement on almost every point. Millie was left to sort through the events of her visit with Aunt Wealthy. *"People who are afraid do terrible things . . . You must be very careful, Millie."* As she remembered her aunt's words, a tiny worm of fear wiggled in her stomach. *Would Mamma and Pappa have sent me if they knew the changing situation in the South? And if I have to be careful about what I say to Uncle Horace, then who can I trust? Aunt Wealthy seemed in her right mind when she gave me the warning. But what about the possibility that she was not?* Millie was determined to pen a letter to her mother at the first stop.

The afternoon air had lost its bite. The rocking of the coach and the drone of voices must have lulled her to sleep. Millie woke with a cough in her throat. She reached in the pocket of the coat beside her for a handkerchief, but pulled out the strange doily Aunt Wealthy had snatched from her windowsill instead. It wasn't a doily at all, but an old piece of net like Ru used to pull catfish from the river. "Eeeek!" Millie threw it out the window and wiped her hand on her skirt.

"What on earth was that?" Uncle Horace asked, offering his clean white handkerchief.

Millie accepted it gratefully. "Just a scrap Aunty left in her pocket." *No wonder Aunt Wealthy has employed a maid, if she's begun leaving such things in odd places around the house.* Millie couldn't help but think of Mrs. Lightcap again; one day her mind was clear as well water, and the next she put the sugar in the linen drawer and set fire to the couch.

That evening when they stopped, Millie took a pen in hand to compose the letter she had been thinking about all day. She found it harder to express her fears than she had imagined. She wished once again that there was some way to keep a letter completely private. She longed to spill out her heart to her mother.

If she were a princess, a president, or a king, she would have used wax and a seal, and then had the letter hand-delivered by messenger. But a stiff lump of sealing wax would break off the moment the letter was put in a satchel with other letters, and that was the fate of letters handed to the postal service. The contents were open to anyone curious enough to unfold and read it. Aunt Wealthy's feelings and reputation were at stake.

Millie toyed with the idea of gluing the pages together, but decided that not only would the glue damage the pages when Mamma tried to pry them apart, but the mere fact of the letter being glued would cause such curiosity that someone was sure to pry it open to find out why. She finally had to settle with the fact that her correspondence, once it left her hand, was open for the world to read, and that any portion of Aunt Wealthy's business she wrote about may as well have been shouted to the world.

Millie chose her words carefully, making no mention of Aunt Wealthy's fears of the situation in the southern states. Mamma and Pappa would only worry. She read the letter over once to herself before she folded it in half and wrote the address on the outside. Millie set it on the dressing table while she applied Aunt Wealthy's balm to her chest. It was sweet-smelling, almost like perfume, and soothed her mind even more than her cough. She slept well, and posted her letter the next morning before they booked passage on a steamboat along the Ohio River to Pittsburgh.

The passengers on the boat were more congenial than any others Millie had met on the trip. She and Uncle Horace shared the captain's table with four middle-aged cousins. In lilting southern voices they introduced themselves as Miz Opal, Miz Ruth, Miz Magnolia, and Mrs. Bliss. Mrs. Bliss, who the cousins all called "Dearest," wore widow's weeds, and when Millie offered her condolences, she accepted them solemnly, dabbing a tear.

Miz Magnolia leaned toward Millie and whispered, "It's all right. She's been a widow for fourteen years now and has long since remarried." She must have seen Millie's questioning look because she continued, still in a whisper. "She married the undertaker who buried her first three husbands. He asked her just after the third funeral. Dearest swore she would never give up grieving for her dearly departeds, but Mr. Bliss—that is his name, you see—said that was perfectly all right, as it promotes business. He must have been right, for his funeral parlor has been very profitable ever since. Dearest has always had a dash of the theatrical about her. We all help now, of course. Mr. Blessed Bliss's Funeral Home puts on lovely funerals."

"*Blessed* Bliss?" Millie couldn't help but smile.

"With a name like that an undertaker needs all the help he can get, don't you agree?" said Dearest, who had apparently heard the whole conversation.

The cousins were clearly of the trade class, and Uncle Horace, while not seeming to avoid them, managed to sit on the opposite side of the boat whenever they were on deck, which, since the weather had turned fine, was as often as Millie could persuade him to accompany her. The air was so much more invigorating, and the countryside and passengers entertaining as well. Millie soon realized that the ancient man with spectacles and mutton chops, who engaged in calisthenics and breathing exercises just after sunup each day, was attached to the cousins in an avuncular way. They referred to him as "Colonel Peabody," but Millie was never quite sure what he was a colonel of, or why he never joined them at the captain's table. From the conversation at meal times, Millie gathered that they were returning home to North Carolina from a family reunion and tour.

One morning as Millie was preparing for her daily study of the Bible, Uncle Horace asked for a moment of her time. "There is something I must discuss with you before you meet my wife, Isabel," he said. "I would rather you say nothing to her about your parents' circumstances."

"Circumstances?"

"Loss of fortune," Uncle Horace clarified.

Millie's face grew very hot.

"Your parents are both of fine old families," Uncle Horace continued. "And I think quite as much of them and you as if you were still rolling in wealth. But Isabel has led a sheltered life. It has been my privilege to keep her from the harsher realities, and I believe I have done well. It would make us more comfortable all around if she is left to suppose that your mother is still in possession of the fortune she once had."

"I cannot act a lie, Uncle. And poverty is not a disgrace," said Millie.

"Of course, good families who have lost their wealth should not consider it a disgrace. There can always be a change of fortune."

"I believe we should look at a person's character, not their family tree or circumstances," Millie said.

"Surely you would not want to be an embarrassment to your great-aunt?" Uncle Horace said, trying another tack. "You would not want to make her uncomfortable?"

"No," Millie said carefully. *Does he think my current outfit is an embarrassment then?* "I would not want to be an embarrassment."

"Good!" Uncle Horace said. "You will leave it to me to take care of your expenses, then, without question or remark."

Millie's feelings were hurt and she could feel her temper rising. "I did not say that, Uncle," she replied stiffly. "I will have to think about it. I don't want to burden you. I would not like being more of an expense to you than any ordinary guest."

"As opposed to an extra-ordinary guest?" he said, amused.

Millie blushed again and wished her face would choose one color and keep it. "I . . . I must think and pray about this before I give you an answer. I am inclined to say no," she said, a trace of stubbornness apparent in her tone.

"If God is not too busy, then, please discuss the issue with him and come to a decision before we reach Philadelphia," he said congenially.

Surely he would not have said such a thing to Aunt Wealthy or Mamma or Pappa!

"Oh! I seem to have forgotten my book," he said, apparently not noticing her clenched teeth. "I will be right back."

Millie pulled her Bible from her bag and flipped through the pages to 1 Timothy 4:12, a passage she had read the day before. "Don't let anyone look down on you because you are young, but set an example for the believers in speech, in life, in love, in faith and in purity." *But Uncle Horace does look down on me because of my youth!* she said to herself in frustration. *And he treats my faith as if it were a child's game.* Millie felt insulted and annoyed, and for a few moments she dwelt on those feelings. Then she remembered how far Uncle Horace had traveled to get her—out of concern for *her* health. *I want him to see that my faith is real, Lord. But surely he's not going to see that through my anger and pride.*

Millie focused on the verse before her. *There must be something here that could help.* She read the verse over slowly two more times. *Speech, life, love, faith, and purity. That's it! That's how I can show him! In speech, by saying I am sorry. In life, by living faithfully and humbly before him and God. In love, by accepting Uncle Horace's gift—even if it is offered for reasons that hurt my pride. In faith, by trusting that You, Lord, will help me. And in purity, by confessing my sin to You—which I do right now. Lord, I'm sorry that I was angry and prideful. Please forgive me. And help me tell Uncle Horace I'm sorry, too.*

"Excuse me, miss. I couldn't help but notice your lovely face."

Millie jumped—a little startled to be addressed in such a way by a complete stranger. The young man who had taken Uncle Horace's place had a wide, insincere smile under his mustache. His long hair was neatly parted, and the scent of bay rum hair tonic floated about him like a miasma.

"Please don't think I'm being forward. It is a professional observation, I assure you. I am a seller of a number of incredible beauty products, most notably, 'Dr. Kingsley's Age Reducing Elixir.' " He was speaking with great speed and enthusiasm. "You don't need it now, of course. But think . . . " he directed his glance meaningfully at Mrs. Bliss, who was strolling slowly along the deck, "what the future will bring. Unless your beauty is protected by this amazing elixir, it will fade. Time will steal the roses from your cheeks and the cherry stains from your lips. Ah! You blush! But don't think me forward!" He pulled his case onto his lap, opening it to display his wares. "For only one dollar a bottle, your youthful blush can be protected! How many bottles will you need?"

He looked hopefully at Millie, as if expecting her to pull out her purse and purchase his entire supply. When she didn't say anything, he leaned forward conspiratorially and pointed at the Bible on her lap. "You know what the good Book says: an ounce of prevention is worth a pound of cure. Now, a beautiful woman like yourself is surely . . . "

"That was not a proverb from the Bible, sir," Millie said, finding her voice at last. "But this is: 'Like a gold ring in a pig's snout is a beautiful woman who shows no discretion.' "

A merry laugh made them both look up. Miz Opal was standing over them. "I am delighted to meet someone of your age who is acquainted with God's Word! Well?" she said to the young man. "Are you going to offer me that seat, or must I topple you out of it?"

"Good heavens! Of course, madam!" He picked up his bag quickly, but not quickly enough. Miz Magnolia had spied her cousin speaking with the stranger and pointed it out to the group. Colonel Peabody led the charge across the deck, and Millie found herself completely surrounded, the hapless peddler pushed to the fringe of the group.

"I fear for the manners of our youth," Miz Opal said, lowering herself into the seat and examining Millie. "You have been very quiet at meal times. So quiet that I have not caught your name."

Millie introduced herself. Question followed question, almost faster than she could answer. How old was she? What was her mother's maiden name? The Dinsmores were a very fine family. Did she know that? What was her uncle thinking to leave her on the deck all alone!

"Quiet!" Miz Opal said loudly, and the buzz subsided. "The child's not a June bug at a hen party! Give her a moment to catch her breath!" And then, completely disregarding her own advice, "Would you like to join us? We have commandeered a very comfortable spot on the deck."

Millie agreed, and was escorted to a chair, with another saved for Uncle Horace when he should appear.

"Dinsmore," one of the ladies explained to another, nodding as if that said it all.

"You don't worry about a thing, now," Miz Magnolia said, patting her hand. "We'll take care of you."

Millie wanted to apologize to her uncle as soon as he returned, but the words would not come out. *It's so easy with Mamma and Pappa,* she thought to herself, *but admitting I was wrong to Uncle Horace seems like something else entirely. And with the cousins listening, it's impossible! I'll do it later, Lord. I promise.*

However, Uncle Horace seemed to forget the whole incident just as he had forgotten the argument with Aunt Wealthy—acting as if nothing had happened.

Wounded Pride

The next day, and every day thereafter, the cousins saved a chair for Millie and one for Uncle Horace, too. Although Uncle Horace seemed bored by the ladies' talk, he was content to sit nearby and read his papers.

Millie found the cousins good-hearted, if a little too inquisitive at times. Their friendship was as comfortable and all-encompassing as a goose down comforter. Miz Opal, a strong Christian woman, spent hours talking to Millie and joined in Millie's daily study of the Bible. Opal's cousins, though not much concerned with religion, reminded Millie so much of the ladies of Pleasant Plains that she felt as if she had known them for years. They clucked and fussed over Millie as if she were their own, feeding her honeyed tea if her throat tickled, and making sure that her shawl was warm enough and that her knees were covered.

The cousins spent almost every afternoon playing cards while Colonel Peabody told outrageous stories of derring-do in which he figured largely as the hero. Millie found them by far the most entertaining group on the ship, and often brought her sketchbook to work on while she listened to them talk. Other passengers seemed to agree, lingering on the outskirts and sometimes joining in conversations.

"I never feel quite safe on water," Miz Ruth declared one day. "And steam engines make me nervous. All of that . . . metal. I'm sure it can't be safe."

"Nonsense!" said Colonel Peabody as he set his cards aside. This could only mean that he had a bad hand and did not want to play it, and so would provide a story instead. "Steam engines are quite reliable."

"Can you possibly think so?" asked Miz Ruth.

"I can. I have made it my ambition and goal," he declared to the ladies, "to travel the world by every means of transportation invented by God or man. I have ridden racehorses in India and traveled by camel across the Sahara. I have floated over Paris in a combustible gas-filled balloon the size of an ocean vessel."

"Why would they fill an ocean vessel with combustible gas?" Miz Ruth asked.

Colonel Peabody removed his glasses and polished them.

"The balloon was filled with gas, dear," Miz Opal explained.

"Oh my!" Miz Ruth fanned herself. "Imagine that!"

Uncle Horace lowered his paper a fraction and looked at Millie over the top, one eyebrow cocked as if to say "nonsense!" Several passengers, not sharing Uncle Horace's opinions, had stopped to listen to the conversation.

"In the mines of India," the Colonel declared, noticing his expanded audience, "I rode on a wooden ore cart pulled along a track by reptiles — giant alligators, if you could call the monsters that."

"Psh-ha-ha-*hornswaggle*," Uncle Horace exploded behind his paper.

"Bless you!" Colonel Peabody said.

"Quite so," Uncle Horace agreed. Millie wished desperately for a fan to hide her smile. She had to settle for blinking her eyes very hard and biting her lip. She thought she had achieved success until she noticed that the face cream peddler had weaseled his way into a seat on the Colonel's left, and was blinking furiously back at her. Millie felt the flush creeping up her face. Miz Opal looked from Millie's red cheeks to the young man and narrowed her eyes. The peddler developed a sudden fascination for the Colonel, who had switched from ships and boats to steam locomotives. This was a subject of great interest to Millie, as they would be taking the train from Pittsburgh to Philadelphia. The trip of three hundred miles would have taken at least ten days on the stage. Uncle Horace assured her the distance would be covered in only two days, with one night spent at an inn.

"Steam locomotives are the finest transportation ever devised by man," the Colonel said, warming to his subject. "There are now hundreds of miles of rail stretching across these United States, and I have been over every single mile, at speeds of up to twenty-five miles an hour." His audience murmured in admiration. "Railways are the transportation of the future!"

"I think this mad dash to speed in transportation will end in disaster," Miz Opal said. "We are trifling with things beyond our comprehension. What happens when we reach thirty miles an hour, or faster? We simply do not know what these speeds will do to a human body. Will we be able to breathe? Our lungs may not be strong enough to draw in the atmosphere!"

"I have read accounts of sailors weathering hurricanes," Millie pointed out logically. "They were able to breathe."

"Brilliant point!" the Colonel exclaimed.

"I've heard that vibrations such as those created by the wheels on the track may stop the human heart," Mrs. Bliss offered hopefully.

Colonel Peabody closed his eyes, as if imagining himself on a locomotive. "If my heart must stop, let it be while racing madly down the rails! The extreme speeds make me feel closer to life than death. Although there are dangers in rail travel . . ." He paused, opening his eyes to see what effect his raptures were having.

"What kind of danger?" Mrs. Bliss leaned forward.

Millie's Remarkable Journey

"My most exciting rail trip was aboard the 'Best Friend of Charleston' in 1831. The steam engine exploded, killing the fireman and injuring the engineer."

"Good heavens!" Miz Ruth fanned herself. "I knew they were dangerous!"

"You would have nothing to fear today, dear lady. Assuring the safety of the passengers was quite simple. I wrote the owners immediately, advising them that a flat car should be piled high with bales of cotton and placed between the engine and the passenger cars."

"That was *your* suggestion?" Uncle Horace asked, finally putting his paper aside.

"Well, er," Colonel Peabody blustered, "it may have been made by others as well. . . . At any rate, they rebuilt the engine, renamed it the *Phoenix*, and they are using the flat car until this day."

"I need a little fresh air," Uncle Horace said, standing up. "Would you care for a stroll around the deck, Millie?"

"I do believe I could use a walk, Uncle," Millie said, standing.

When they were out of earshot, Uncle Horace said, "Some people should not be allowed to speak for more than three sentences in a row."

"Pappa once told me that there is no one you cannot learn *something* from," said Millie.

"That is correct. Always listen to your parents," he replied.

"Do you mean you have learned something from Colonel Peabody, Uncle?" Millie asked in surprise.

"Most assuredly. I have learned that I do not enjoy his company."

7

Burning Bustles

*Consider what a great forest
is set on fire by a
small spark.*

JAMES 3:5

Burning Bustles

*M*illie paid special attention to the outfit she chose for their arrival in Pittsburgh. She was still stinging from Uncle Horace's remarks and wanted to be very sure she was not an embarrassment to him. She donned Damaris's best dress, brightened by a paisley shawl and Claudina's dainty ankle boots, and surveyed herself in the mirror. The boot heels gave her two inches in height, and her mother's combs held her hair in a sophisticated twist. But something was missing. She finally settled on Lu's cap, perched at a jaunty angle, to complete the ensemble. *That will do,* Millie thought. *I dare Uncle Horace to be embarrassed by my company!*

She gave her hair one last pat, then started for the door, chin held high. Halfway across the floor her ankle turned slightly, and she lurched like a sailor for two or three steps before she caught her balance. *Walk on your toes. Glide!* That's what Claudina had said. She smoothed her skirt and tried again. *Much better.*

Millie glided out of the room and up the stairs, looking for the Colonel and the four cousins to say her goodbyes. The fivesome, who were staying on board and continuing their journey, planned to travel up the river and then overland by stage, arriving home in North Carolina in a little over a month.

"Don't you look lovely!" Miz Magnolia said, giving Millie a hug.

"Oh!" cried Mrs. Bliss. "You would make a lovely orphan, and you could add such atmosphere by weeping in the front row at a funeral."

Millie's Remarkable Journey

"In a theatrical sense," Miz Opal said, taking Millie's hand reassuringly. "I'm sure Dearest doesn't mean a thing about your own parents. You simply appeal to her sense of the dramatic."

"Of course that's right!" said Mrs. Bliss. "Your parents would be perfectly welcome to attend also. Do they look good in black? They could pose as mysterious mourners from out of town!"

Millie said goodbye to each of her new friends, although she stopped short of promising to attend one of their funerals. The patent medicine peddler, who had come to see what the commotion was about, expressed grief that Millie was leaving the boat and offered her a free sample and his card, both of which Millie graciously declined.

"I'll walk with you," Miz Opal said, as Millie excused herself to find her uncle.

"Now you take care of yourself, young lady," Miz Opal said when they sighted Uncle Horace. "Your health seems somewhat better, at least."

Millie had to agree. By this time last year in Pleasant Plains, she had found herself confined to bed, but here she seemed to be growing stronger each day. "I'm sure it has improved because of your tea," said Millie.

"Or the fact that you are young and sure to get better with good weather and plenty of rest," Miz Opal said, laughing. "Your company on this boat has made the journey brighter for several old ladies. We are not the sort you are likely to find mixing with the Dinsmores," Miz Opal continued, "but we don't live far away. Mr. Bliss's funeral home is in the closest seaport to the Roselands Plantation. Your ship will no doubt dock there, and Blessed Bliss's is a hard establishment to miss. I will be spending some time there with my cousins. If you are ever inclined, do come for a visit."

Millie assured her she would try, and then, after giving her one last hug, she hurried to meet Uncle Horace.

"You look enchanting," Uncle Horace said with a bow, much to her satisfaction. "We shall greet Pittsburgh in style!" He offered his arm and they walked down the gangplank together.

They dined at a fine restaurant and spent an hour sightseeing. *Walking on your toes is elegant*, Millie thought, *until they go numb*. She managed well enough on the smooth sidewalks, and she consoled herself with the fact that most of the day would be spent sitting on the train. Uncle Horace must have noticed the trouble she was having, as he hailed a cabriolet to drive them the short distance to the Pittsburgh and Pennsylvania Central Railroad station when their sightseeing was over. Millie had never been so glad to sit down in all her life.

The steam locomotive puffing on the tracks looked like the baby brother of the monstrous locomotives Ru had pictures of on his bedroom wall. "The engine is smaller than I expected," Millie said.

Uncle Horace agreed. "The tracks here will not withstand the weight of the heavier British machines."

The locomotive itself looked like a huge steel barrel lying sideways on a wagon. There was a firebox attached to the back of the barrel. Puffs of black smoke rose from a tall chimney on the front. As they watched, the puffs turned into a black column reaching up into the blue sky.

"They're heating her up," Uncle Horace said.

"Do we have time to walk around it, Uncle?" Millie was determined to remember the sight, sound, and feel of it so she could describe it to Ru.

Uncle Horace consulted his watch. "I believe so." He offered his arm, a courtesy Millie was glad to accept, as the

ground along the tracks was inches deep in cinders. They made their way to the engine, and stood close enough that they could feel the heat radiating from the firebox.

"How does it work?" asked Millie.

Uncle Horace looked surprised that she would ask. "As I understand it," he said, "coal is burned in the firebox. This produces hot gasses that run through copper fire tubes in the big cylinder—the boiler—and turn water into steam. The water expands with such force that it moves these pistons." He pointed to smaller cylinders on the side of the engine. "The pistons in turn push the arms that turn the wheels."

"An elegant design," Millie marveled. "Just like a blackberry pie."

"Pardon?"

"God makes the parts, we make the pie. We have always had water and coal and fire," explained Millie.

"I believe constructing an engine is a bit more difficult than baking a pie," Uncle Horace said.

"Which is why it took us a bit longer to figure out how to put them together into something marvelous," Millie agreed. "Just imagine what we will be figuring out in a hundred years!"

They continued around the train, examining the coal car just behind the locomotive, and the four passenger cars, which looked very much like wagons with roofs and a bench seat along each side.

"Are you ready to board?" Uncle Horace asked.

"Yes. And thank you for the tour. It is much more impressive to ride on it if you understand its workings, don't you think?"

They returned to the platform where a line had formed waiting for the conductor to allow them aboard. Millie

stood behind a thin woman with a bustle so massive it was hard not to stare, and harder still to get out of the way when she made sudden turns.

"All aboard!" the conductor called, assisting the first passenger, an elderly gentleman, up the three steps from the platform into the car. The line of passengers disappeared into the car one by one.

When it was her turn, Millie practically jumped up the steps into the car, eager to be on board. She had just made the second step when the heel of her boot caught. She lunged forward, hands going out instinctively to break her fall. She caught herself on an upholstered seat and pulled herself upright, only to realize that she had been saved from disaster not by a cushion, but by the bustle of the woman in front of her.

"Outrageous!" the woman said, gathering her skirts.

"I do apologize," Millie said. "But thank heavens you were there. Your . . . ," she suddenly became aware of Uncle Horace behind her and other gentlemen looking on from the half full car, ". . . apparatus saved me from a nasty fall."

"I never!" the woman said, brushing past Millie and taking a seat. Millie turned the other way, but all of the seats were full. She was forced to choose one not very far from the offended woman.

Millie was a little disappointed at the interior of the train car. It was rather plain, much like an enclosed dray. There were wooden seats — totally lacking in upholstery, Millie noted with dismay — along each of the long walls, and windows that were now shut, but could be opened.

"That is a bad idea, madam," Uncle Horace said. Millie looked up. The woman she'd secretly nicknamed "Mrs. Bustle" had opened a window. "When the train starts to move," Uncle Horace explained, "the force of the air will push the smoke and cinders right down on these cars. You will want to keep your window up."

The woman pointedly ignored him.

She is humiliated, thought Millie. *I offended her pride, so she won't listen to good advice.* A twang like a fiddle string plucked Millie's heart. *Pride. Uncle Horace offended my pride, so I didn't take his advice. I still need to confess my pride to him and apologize. But waiting just a little longer can't hurt.*

The train started forward, causing several passengers to take seats hastily. The metallic clickity-clack of the wheels on the rails grew louder and faster as the train gained speed. Millie had to agree with Colonel Peabody's assessment—it was thrilling.

The air in the crowded car grew warm, and several passengers opened more windows, willing to risk the smoke and cinders to escape the heat of the crowded car. The occasional cinders that spun through windows were cause for constant diligence. Millie saw one burn a hole through a gentleman's sleeve before he could shake it off and grind it out with his boot.

Millie looked at her uncle. *He doesn't seem to be worried about my answer. Maybe I don't have to apologize after all. Uncle Horace doesn't know what the Holy Spirit spoke to my heart, and I asked God for forgiveness. That was the important part. Uncle Horace would never understand anyway.*

"Gooobers, gooo-ber peas!" a small boy called as he walked through the car holding up his wares aloft. Uncle Horace bought Millie a bag of peanuts. She thanked him pleasantly. Cracking peanuts was a very satisfactory occupation in her present mood.

She looked up to see Mrs. Bustle rising from her seat. Millie thought for a moment that the woman was coming to

speak to her, but she walked past, intent on the peddler. At that moment, a cinder spun in the window, catching on Millie's arm. She jerked, and the glowing ember bounced, landing right on the enormous bustle and settling into the folds. Millie blinked. *Maybe I won't have to say anything. Maybe the spark will go out by itself.*

She watched the bustle carefully for a few moments, glancing at it from the corner of her eye, so as not to appear to be staring. She was relieved when there was no further sign of the ember. The woman followed the vendor down the car, and Millie sighed with relief. The spark must have died out in the depths of the fabric. Millie went back to cracking her peanuts, glancing up a few moments later as the woman walked past again on the way to her seat. *Is that a wisp of smoke rising from that billowing contraption? It can't be. But still . . .*

"Excuse me," Millie said loudly. "Madam, your . . . "

At that moment the bustle burst into flames.

"Good heavens!" cried Uncle Horace, leaping to his feet and starting to bat the flames with his bare hands. The woman, unaware of the danger to her person, spun to confront her attacker. The bustle, a positive conflagration now, swung within inches of the face of the woman in the seat opposite Millie, who screamed. Mrs. Bustle, alerted to her danger at last, screamed as well and started to run. Millie grabbed Uncle Horace's coat from the seat beside her, raced after the woman, and dropped it over the fire, throwing herself on the bustle and hugging it to smother the flames.

"Hip-hip, hurrah!" Millie turned to face a car full of cheering passengers. She didn't feel heroic at all standing next to the weeping woman. Uncle Horace offered Mrs.

Millie's Remarkable Journey

Bustle his coat to tie round her waist. Millie helped her to her seat.

"I am so sorry," Millie said, starting to explain about the ember.

"Oh, leave me alone!" the poor woman wailed. Millie had no choice but to return to her seat.

"Traveling with you is almost as exciting as traveling with Eva and Wealthy," Uncle Horace said, handing Millie her hat, which had come off during the scuffle. "I may be getting too old for this. Did you get soot on your dress?"

"No, Uncle. I'm afraid your coat was ruined, however."

"Ah, well, it was given up to a noble cause. But it would be a shame to ruin your becoming dress or lovely shawl."

Millie stared at her pale reflection in the glass of the window as she adjusted her hat. *Is Uncle Horace complimenting me because he knows my feelings were hurt on the boat, or does he really think my dress and shawl are lovely? I know Mamma says it doesn't matter what people think, Jesus. But it does matter to me — at least a little. I can't help it. Only what You think matters more.* She leaned toward the window, looking into the reflection of her own eyes. *What do You see, Jesus?* She suddenly felt that terrible twang again, deep inside. *Pride. That's what You see. Lying hidden in my heart. Forgive me, Lord.*

"Uncle?" she said.

"Yes, Millie."

"I would like to accept your offer."

"Offer?" He looked puzzled.

"To cover my expenses. I'm sorry I was angry with you. I did pray about it that day, and God's Holy Spirit convicted me of pride. I shouldn't have spoken to you the way I did. I told God that I would apologize, but I didn't do it — until now. It has been just like the ember that caused that fire, Uncle. I did not obey right away, and it has given pride an opportunity to smoulder in my heart."

Uncle Horace looked at her solemnly.

What is he thinking? thought Millie. *Does he have any idea how hard it was to confess that? To tell him what was in my heart?*

"God speaks to you through burning bustles?" he asked at last.

Millie could only nod. *Well, that certainly takes care of my pride! I'm sure I haven't a shred left.*

<hr />

Millie was very glad to leave the train in Rockville, where the passengers cheered her once more as she disembarked. They spent the evening and night at the station hotel, and in the morning boarded a train on the Pennsylvania Line to Philadelphia. Millie was more excited about the visit to Philadelphia than she could express. It was not only the birthplace of liberty, it was the second largest city in the nation. Artists, writers, and thinkers . . . they all came to Philadelphia. Audubon himself had a small plantation just twenty miles from town.

There were people on the streets even at the late hour the train pulled in, though the shop windows were darkened. Millie noticed a spring in Uncle Horace's step as they approached the hotel. She could have sworn he was smiling when they stepped into the soft gaslight of the hotel lobby. She could not help but smile herself, thinking of the times when her Pappa had come home from a business trip. Her Mamma was always waiting for him, and the children could hardly wait to be called out of hiding to jump on their Pappa. *Uncle Horace must have missed his wife and children terribly for the last several weeks. No wonder I've never seen him smile. Yet he came all the way to Indiana to get me anyway. He does have a good heart.*

Uncle Horace gave his name, and the clerk provided a key.

"Mrs. Dinsmore has been here a few weeks," he said. The Dinsmores had rented a family suite, complete with dining room, sitting room, and bedroom. Uncle Horace led the way up plush carpeted stairs, turned the key, and pushed open the door. Millie waited a polite moment to give his family a chance to greet him before she entered, but when she stepped into the room, Uncle Horace was standing alone in the middle of the floor.

A black woman dozed in a rocking chair in the corner of the room, snoring softly. Millie tried to close the door quietly, but the black woman jerked awake.

"Master Horace!" she said, trying to pretend she had not been sleeping at all. "The missus told me to wait up for you. She's gone to bed, and the children, too."

"Very well, Jonati. You may go to bed as well," he said. His smile was gone and the corners of his mouth tightened—as if they refused to admit that a smile had ever been there at all.

CHAPTER

A Work of Art

Therefore, this is what the Lord says: You have not obeyed me; you have not proclaimed freedom for your fellow countrymen.

JEREMIAH 34:17

A Work of Art

*M*illie bid Uncle Horace a good night and practically collapsed into bed, but thoughts of him, combined with her cough, kept her from sleep. Aunt Wealthy's ointment did relieve the cough, but only prayer could ease her hurt for Uncle Horace. She awoke the next morning to find Jonati bustling about her room.

"You better wake up, miss," the woman said. "Breakfast be in half an hour, and that's not enough time to make you decent. I prepared your things. I'd have done it last night, but Master Horace sent me to bed. You heard him."

"You didn't have to do that," Millie said, sitting up. She was shocked to see by the clock on the wall that it was past ten.

"Wash up," Jonati said. "I'll do your hair."

"I can do it myself," Millie said kindly. "You don't need to wait on me." She rose and extended her hand. "I don't believe we have been introduced. My name is Millie Keith."

Jonati took her hand gingerly. "I don't know where you come from, child, but it's not from around here."

"Indiana," Millie said.

"Hmmm," said Jonati, folding her arms. "Figures Mr. Horace would drag home a wild Indiana-girl who don't know how civilized people behave. Well, I'm going to tell you how. You sit down while I do your hair. And don't be settin' no bad example for my children. They have enough trouble mindin' as it is."

Millie found herself seated while the woman used a brush none too gently on her long hair. She allowed herself to be dressed in her best green and black silk and her hair pinned up. It took twice as long as it would have for Millie to dress herself. Jonati grumbled the whole time, never addressing Millie directly, but finding fault with the fit of her dress and the polish on her shoes.

"That's all I can do," the nursemaid said at last. "But I don't know what the missus is going to think."

"Thank you for trying, anyway," Millie said, edging past the woman and escaping into the hall. The Dinsmores were waiting for her at the table.

"Forgive me," Millie said, surveying the faces. "I was very tired and must have overslept."

"We have not quite expired of hunger," said Isabel Dinsmore, who could only be described as a beauty. Her skin was the texture of porcelain, tinted with rose and cream. Her large blue eyes were spangled with thick lashes. She hardly looked old enough to be the mother of the children seated around her. Uncle Horace, on the opposite side of the table, gazed at his wife as if she were a treasure. *He loves her*, Millie thought. *And he is proud of her beauty.*

The Dinsmore children were easy to identify. Uncle Horace had spoken of them often enough. Adelaide, who was twelve, had her mother's grace, but her father's thoughtful expression. Lora, ten, and Louise, eight, looked much as their mother must have at their age. Arthur, a plump, ringleted fellow of six, had obviously not been patient while they waited—he had jelly on his fingers and cheeks. Walter, who was four, examined Millie with wide, solemn eyes when Uncle Horace introduced her. "Plethed to meet you," he said with a lisp. Baby Enna, who was just two, hid her face in her nursemaid's shoulder.

"And I'm pleased to meet you all," said Millie when the introductions were finished. "I have been missing my own brothers and sisters in Pleasant Plains, so I hope you don't mind spending some time with me." Millie paused to cough discreetly into her napkin.

"What's wrong with her?" Arthur asked.

"Her lungs have been damaged by frontier air," Isabel said. "It is wholly unsuitable for young ladies."

"But she has improved already, simply by breathing our civilized atmosphere," Uncle Horace added. "And she will be quite well by the time we send her home."

"I want to know all about Pleasant Plains and cousin Zillah," Adelaide said. "She's my age, isn't she?"

"Zillah is not our real cousin, and neither is she," Louise said, as Millie was seated. "Our cousin would never look like *that*."

All the children looked at Millie now, the younger ones in some confusion, and the older ones obviously measuring her. *What can the child mean? My hair is brushed and my face is clean. Jonati made certain of that. Perhaps there is something horrid hanging from my nose?* She clasped her hands in her lap to keep from rubbing it just to make sure.

"Now, Louise," Isabel said. "You can't be expected to keep up with fashions in Indiana. She is reasonably pretty, and once she is properly outfitted, it will be very entertaining to introduce her to our friends. No one else will have a girl from the frontier at their parties!"

"Have you ever westled a beaw?" Walter asked.

"No, but I saw a dancing bear once. It wore a dress and hopped about on its hind feet. It was quite ridiculous." *And at this moment, I know exactly how the poor bear felt,* thought Millie.

"What are we supposed to call her, Mother?" Arthur asked. "And what does she call us?"

Millie's Remarkable Journey

Isabel took a sip of tea while she considered. "Having a step-niece of this age would not reflect badly on my own age, would it Horace?"

"Of course not," he said.

"Then she may call me aunt," Isabel decided. "And you children may call her cousin."

"Thank you, my dear," said Uncle Horace, smiling at his wife.

"Since she is not the sort one need feel ashamed of, I've no objection to it," Isabel said.

What would have happened if I had been wall-eyed and buck-toothed, Millie wondered. *Would she have sent me back to Pleasant Plains? Or simply put a barrel over my head?*

A house servant brought a large covered tray and set it in the middle of the table. He removed the lid, revealing piles of scrambled eggs, ham, and kippers, and began serving the family plate-by-plate, beginning with Uncle Horace.

"Thank you," Millie said when he set her food in front of her.

Louise laughed out loud, and Arthur covered his mouth. The servant acted as if he had not heard her. When the plates were served, Millie bowed her head and folded her hands.

"What is she doing, Father?" Arthur asked.

"Praying," Uncle Horace said.

"Like we do at church? Why?" asked Arthur.

"Because that is the custom in her family. And I expect you to respect it while she stays with us," he said, giving them a very stern look. Millie was desperately glad she had practiced praying in front of Uncle Horace on the trip, or her tongue would have been frozen.

A Work of Art

"Dear Father in heaven," she said. "We thank You for this meal. We thank You for the glorious day You have created, and ask Your blessings on each member of this family. Amen."

"Are we going to have to do that every time we eat?" Arthur asked. His father gave him another look.

"I suppose you have a great deal of shopping to do, Millie," Isabel said. "I'm sure I do not feel equal to the exertion."

"Are you not well?" Uncle Horace asked in concern.

"Travel wearies me. And I have been left all alone with the children for weeks."

"I thought you liked shopping. Surely there are a few pretty things you need for yourself," said Uncle Horace as if he were coaxing a child.

"I may be able to manage it if I have Miss Worth's help. You expect her today, do you not? It's so inconvenient that she is not here now. You shouldn't have allowed her to go at all, leaving me alone with the servants and children, Horace. It was selfish and inconsiderate."

"But dear," he said. "It would have been very hard for her to come back here without spending time with her family. She hasn't seen them in a year."

"Her employment is more important, surely," she said. The conversation went on like this for some time. Isabel apparently had a storehouse of complaints that she had saved up for her husband's return.

"Excuse me," Millie said at last. "If we are to go shopping, perhaps I should get ready?"

"Of course," Uncle Horace said.

Millie hurried to her room, glanced around to make sure Jonati wasn't waiting to jump out at her with a hairbrush, and then shut the door behind her. She walked straight to the mirror and examined her nose, then inspected the rest of her person. She was glad to see the very same Millie Keith that greeted her every morning. Suddenly, she burst out laughing. *If I were a muskrat, Gordon would say I was just the muskrat God meant me to be! It's a good thing You warned me about my pride, Lord, if I am going to spend four months with the Dinsmores! Four months! It somehow seems much longer than it did before.*

Millie sat on her bed trying to sort her thoughts. *Honor your father and mother. It means bringing them honor by the way you act and by the decisions you make. Help me, Jesus,* Millie prayed. *Help me to honor my parents, and most of all, to honor You.*

Millie chose her prettiest bonnet, and then pulled her Mamma's India shawl from the trunk and wrapped it around her. The heavy silk smelled of lavender perfume, and the weight settled on her shoulders like a hug. "Don't worry, Mamma," Millie said out loud. "I know what Jesus thinks of me, and that's all that really matters!"

"That took you long enough," Isabel said when Millie reappeared.

"No matter," said Uncle Horace, jumping to his feet. "It gave me time to order a carriage. Are any of the children coming?"

"Adelaide, Louise, and Lora. Jonati has taken the younger ones out," replied Isabel.

The three little girls came in at that moment and Millie nearly gasped. They looked like walking sugarplums, iced with ribbons and bows. Their hair hung in fat sausage curls, and they had so many layers of lace pantalets that their tiny shoes were completely covered. They looked curiously at Millie's simple attire.

A Work of Art

"What a fright of a bonnet. I don't want her going with us if she's going to wear *that*," Louise said.

"Now, now," said her mother. "We'll hide her in the carriage and drive directly to the milliner's shop where she can purchase a handsome one."

"What a pretty shawl, cousin," exclaimed Adelaide. Millie smiled, grateful for the compliment.

The drive to the milliner's was so short that Millie thought they might as well have walked. She would have loved to lean out the window for a better view of the city, but restrained herself lest she mortify her friends by an exhibition of her unfashionable headgear. Louise exited the coach and dashed for the door of the shop, apparently loath to be seen on the street with Millie. Uncle Horace held the door for the ladies, and Millie was the last to enter.

"Now don't worry about the cost," Uncle Horace said under his breath as Millie went past.

The milliner's shop was larger than the grandest store in Pleasant Plains or Lansdale. There were hats along each wall and on a forest of hat trees scattered about the room. A bevy of cheerful young women descended on Isabel immediately, obviously recognizing a frequent customer. Millie waited quietly as Isabel pointed out several hats that she wanted to try on, demanding the full attention of Uncle Horace and both shop girls. When those hats were all rejected and a new batch requested, Millie wandered across the room to a wall of plumed and feathered hats. There were hats with wings, hats with tail feathers spread, and one that resembled a nest holding three blue robin's eggs. Millie recognized peacock and pheasant feathers as well as some from doves and hummingbirds. There were others so brightly colored that Millie was sure they must have been dyed. She took a hat with a complete bird nesting on the crown down off the wall and tried it on, posing in front of the looking glass, her arms spread like branches.

> *Woodman, spare that tree! she quoted.*
> *Touch not a single bough!*
> *In youth it sheltered me,*
> *And I'll protect it now.*
> *'Twas my forefather's hand*
> *That placed it near his cot;*
> *There, woodman, let it stand,*
> *Thy axe shall harm it not!*

Adelaide's reflection gaped at her from the mirror.

"My rendition of a poem by George Pope Morris. I cannot remember the next line. This hat does not really suit me, does it?" Millie turned for a side view.

Adelaide giggled.

"You are right," Millie sighed, putting it back on the shelf. "I suppose I shall have to try others." She paused beside a tree of plain hats and bonnets with wide brims. Millie loved wide, floppy hats. She tried one on and thought it very becoming. "What do you think, Adelaide?"

"Very fine for travel, or walking in the country, perhaps," Adelaide said in a whisper, "but you should get something more elegant as well, cousin."

"I would appreciate your opinion," Millie whispered back. "Which would you suggest?"

With Adelaide's help she chose several, including a handsome cap of periwinkle blue that would look stunning on Lu. "I'm going to need an entire trunk just to carry my hats home," Millie laughed.

A Work of Art

When the selections were made, Uncle Horace paid the clerk and gave him the address of the hotel. Millie stored her old bonnet in a hatbox and chose a cap that suited her dress. Millie couldn't help but be aware of how the cap set off her eyes and framed her oval face. It was lovely, and Louise must have agreed because she deigned to walk beside Millie on the way to the carriage.

Their next visit was to a fashionable shoe store where Isabel fitted herself and her children with several pairs each, and suggested that Millie buy shoes for the house, heavy walking shoes, and dancing slippers. There were ample salesmen, and Millie was waited on hand and foot. Shoes were carried out for her approval, and style suggestions were made. The shoes, like the hats, were sent to the hotel.

"You will, of course, need a pair of gaiters to match each handsome dress you have made," Isabel said as they re-entered the carriage. "But I am far too fatigued to shop more today. Horace, I must return to the hotel." There was no persuading her otherwise, although Uncle Horace did try.

Miss Worth, a serious-looking woman in her mid-thirties, was awaiting them when they returned to their parlor.

"So you are here at last!" Isabel greeted her. "Are you quite ready to take charge of the children? You know they give me a headache."

"Yes, Mrs. Dinsmore," the governess said.

"I trust your family was well, Miss Worth?" Uncle Horace inquired.

"Very. And how did you find your relations, Mr. Dinsmore?"

"I used a map," Uncle Horace said. "Fortunately the cartographer was quite accurate." No one but Millie laughed. *Poor Uncle Horace,* she thought. *No wonder he never smiles.*

Millie's Remarkable Journey

"I am going to lie down until it is time to dress for dinner," Isabel said, "and would advise you to do the same, Millie." She excused herself. Millie lingered long enough to be formally introduced to the governess, and then went to her room and threw herself on the bed.

Millie was roused by a knock at the door. *How long have I been sleeping?* She hurried to the door, expecting to find Jonati scolding her for being tardy to dinner, only to find a porter with an armful of brown paper parcels. "Are you sure you haven't made a mistake?" Millie asked in surprise. "I have already received my purchases."

"No mistake, miss. Room 95, see? And here's the name on the note and the bundles."

"Millie Keith," she read. "Well then. Please bring them in."

The man laid the packages down, and Millie waited until the door was shut behind him before she tore open the card. "My dear niece," it read. "Please excuse the liberty I have taken in having Miss Worth select the fabric for your dresses. I did not want to put undue strain on you or my lovely wife. Hoping they may suit your taste, your affectionate uncle, H.D."

There were materials for five beautiful dresses—a sage colored merino, fine and soft; an all wool delaine in royal purple with an embroidered sprig; and three silks, black, dark brown, and silver gray, each rich and heavy enough to almost stand alone. There was also a box of kid gloves—one or two pairs to match each dress, and the rest white for evening wear. The last parcel contained trimming for the dresses—ribbons, buttons, and heavy silk fringes. Nothing had been forgotten. Miss Worth, it seemed, had excellent, if extravagant, taste.

A Work of Art

There came another rap at the door. Millie opened it to find Uncle Horace standing outside.

"May I come in?" he asked.

"Uncle, you are too kind," Millie said seriously. "You have spent far too much, much more than you would on an ordinary guest, I'm sure."

"It is as much for Isabel's comfort as your own," he said with a shrug. "You are seeing Isabel in a very difficult time. She has been all alone with the children and servants for weeks. I am sure you held your tongue more than once at the breakfast table, and I wanted to thank you." Millie was terribly pleased that he had noticed. "And I wanted to thank you for not mentioning the fact that I am paying for your purchases."

"You have nothing to thank me for, Uncle. I owe you a great deal for your kindness. May I ask you something, though?"

"Of course."

"Would I be an embarrassment to you if I wore only my hand-me-downs?" she asked.

His face became so thoughtful that Millie was sure he was telling the truth when he replied, "No. Your breeding shows through clearly in your character. You are an honor to the Stanhope name."

"My character is not due to breeding," Millie said. "The Bible says in the first chapter of John that 'to all who receive him, to those who believed in his name, he gave the right to become children of God—children born not of natural descent, nor of human decision or a husband's will, but born of God.' I believe I owe any good that exists in me to God."

Uncle Horace shook his head. "Your fine character almost persuades me that there is something to your religion. Dinner

133

Millie's Remarkable Journey

is to be served for the whole family in our own parlor, and it is probably on the table now. May I escort you?"

Dinner was on the table, and as they entered, the family was in the act of taking their places about it. Miss Worth, the governess, was with them. Her manners were unobtrusive and she was very quiet and reserved.

Millie bowed her head and this time the Dinsmore children made no comments about the prayer. She suspected her Uncle had spoken to them before he came to get her.

"Miss Worth has been telling me about the materials for your dresses, Millie," remarked Isabel, who seemed in a much better mood after her nap. "I think from her description they must be very handsome."

"They are very handsome indeed!" Millie answered. "I don't think I could possibly have been better suited. Thank you so much for choosing them, Miss Worth. You have excellent taste."

Miss Worth looked up in surprise, a smile lighting her face. "You are welcome, Miss Keith."

Isabel laughed. "I don't see that one should be thanked for performing their duties, Millie. That is what her pay is for. Rather, you should thank those who provide that pay."

Millie opened her mouth to reply, but before she could frame the words she wanted, Uncle Horace interrupted.

"I was just thinking that I would love to attend a concert this evening," he said. "Would that be acceptable to you, my dear?"

"How thoughtless of you, Horace," Mrs. Dinsmore replied. "I am sure Millie must be much too fatigued by her journey to think of going out."

"I doubt that our niece from the wild frontier is the least fatigued by shopping," he said laughing. "What do you say, Millie?"

"I did have a nap this afternoon," Millie said, trying not to offend her host or hostess. "It refreshed me wonderfully."

"That's settled then," he said, tossing his napkin onto the table. "Will you attend with us, dear?"

"No," Isabel said, resuming her pout. "I do not feel equal to the exertion."

"How about you, Miss Worth? Jonati can put the children to bed. Will you come?"

Miss Worth looked up hopefully. "I would love to. I adore concerts, and it's been ages since I have attended one."

"You remind me how wonderful they can be, Miss Worth," Isabel said. "Perhaps I can find the fortitude to accompany you, dear."

"Marvelous!" Uncle Horace beamed. "We will make an evening of it! Ready yourself, my dear wife and niece, and you too, Miss Worth."

"Shall we walk or ride," queried Uncle Horace, looking at Millie. "It's only about four city blocks."

Millie replied brightly, "I'd love to wa— "

"We will take the carriage, of course," interrupted Isabel. "What can you be thinking of, Horace? You may be excused to dress, Millie."

"Dress?" Millie said in dismay. "Truthfully, Aunt Isabel, I have nothing more suitable to wear than what I have on." She smoothed the skirts of the green and black dress she had been wearing all day.

"Surely that dress is neat-fitting and pretty enough for any occasion," Uncle Horace said quickly.

Millie's Remarkable Journey

"It will do," sniffed Isabel, "so long as you wear your shawl, and don't throw it back. That collar is hopelessly out of style."

Out of style! Millie had to restrain herself from sniffing right back at the woman. *I sewed this dress not a week before, from the latest pattern!* she retorted silently.

"The concert hall will be crowded and warm," Uncle Horace said.

"Then she can take a fan," Isabel said shortly. "I'll lend her one that I'll not be ashamed to see her carry."

Millie was glad she could say she had a pretty fan of her own and would not need to borrow one, and that she would doubtless be able to refrain from throwing back her shawl in a way to exhibit the unfashionable make of her dress.

When Isabel declared herself ready, Uncle Horace kissed little Enna and patted the other children on the head, bidding them to mind their nursemaid. The party of four made its way to the lobby of the hotel and almost to the front door before Isabel began to sob.

"What's wrong?" Uncle Horace asked, stopping in alarm.

"I can't go!" she cried.

"Why ever not, dear?" he asked patiently.

She leaned pitifully on his arm. "It's the children," she said. "I can't bear to think of the little things left alone with only Jonati to look after them. Oh, it's the stress of having cared for them almost alone these last few weeks, I know. But I simply cannot enjoy the concert this way. I must stay."

"That is not necessary," Uncle Horace said, glancing at Miss Worth.

"Of course, sir," the governess said, her shoulders only drooping a little. She turned and walked back up the stairs.

A Work of Art

Millie did not enjoy the concert at all, or even the dazzling extravagance of the concert hall, or the finery of the patrons. She kept thinking of poor Miss Worth, sitting in the hotel parlor alone after the children had been put to bed. Isabel Dinsmore's theatrics had been quite intentional and timed for the greatest effect, Millie was sure. And she was just as sure that Uncle Horace had believed her every sob, flutter, and sigh. Millie was glad to return to the privacy of her own room and the comfort of God's Word before she went to bed.

Isabel was not inclined to get out of bed at all the next day, complaining of a headache. Uncle Horace had business to attend to, but suggested a morning in the park for the children so their mother could rest. To Millie's delight, he suggested that they walk. He would accompany them as far as the square, and then meet them when his business was done.

Millie gathered up her sketchbook and charcoal, a comfortable hat with a wide brim, and her walking shoes. Uncle Horace was waiting at the door, his silver-tipped cane in hand. "Come, children!" he called out. Miss Worth ushered them all into the hall.

The streets and sidewalks of Philadelphia were crowded. Everyone seemed to be in a hurry to get somewhere. The city even seemed to like to eat on its feet, as food vendors pushed carts up and down the streets.

"Hot corn!" called a young woman with a pushcart. "Here's your nice hot corn! Smoking hot! Piping hot! Oh what beauties I have got!" Her voice was drowned out by the bellow of a man on a wagon: "My hoss is blind and he's got no tail. When he's put in prison, I'll go his bail! Yeddy go, sweet potatoes, oh! Fif-en-ny bit a half peck!" Each street vendor had a call all their own, from the fishmongers to the tinker.

"Terruble Disaster strikes!" a newsboy bellowed by Millie's elbow, waving a newspaper toward her.

"What was the disaster?" Millie asked.

"Buy the paper and find out," the scamp said, shoving it behind his back and placing a dirty bare foot on the head-line of the stack at his feet so she could not read it.

"I'm afraid I have no money," Millie said, starting to walk on.

"It's 'orrible!" the boy said. "You don't want to miss it! Just a fip!"

"Did you forget your money, Millie? I'll buy it for you." Adelaide dug a fip from her purse and handed it to him in exchange for the thin paper. The "Terruble Disaster" turned out to be a collision between a milk wagon and a melon cart. Millie laughed. "Well, he was quite a sales-man!"

Then they turned a corner and a wide red brick building stood before them, just across a spacious square. A tall white bell tower rose from the center of the building. Independence Hall. A thrill shot through Millie.

She thought of old Mr. Tittlebaum, standing on a plat-form in Pleasant Plains two years ago. She could still hear the pride in his voice. "I remember how old I was when the United States of America was born," he had said. This was the place. This was where America was born just sixty years ago. "Be roused and alarmed to stand forth in our just and glorious cause," Mr. Tittlebaum had cried, reciting the

A Work of Art

call to revolution. "Join . . . march on; this shall be your warrant: play the man for God, and for the cities of our God! May the Lord of Hosts, the God of the armies of Israel, be your leader." It still gave Millie chills to remember his speech.

The children were clamoring for candy and sarsaparilla. Uncle Horace produced money for the treats and gave it to Miss Worth. "There is a shop on the corner. I'll leave you here and meet you in an hour."

"Do you mind if I wait here?" Millie asked. "I would like to sketch the building."

Miss Worth did not mind, and after rounding up Arthur, who was throwing rocks at a stray cat, led the children away. Millie walked closer to the building, so close in fact that she feared she would lose perspective for her drawing.

An ancient man with long gray wisps of hair was feeding the pigeons. *Had he known John Adams, George Washington, Benjamin Franklin?* Millie sat on a bench not far from him and started to sketch, including him in her picture. She worked on the outline of the building for some time, and then on the trees surrounding it. She was busy with her final shading when a voice startled her.

"I said hello?" An attractive woman perhaps thirty years old, very simply dressed, was standing a few feet away, looking at her.

"Hello," Millie said. "I am afraid I was absorbed in my art."

"I'll buy it from you if it is any good," the woman said, stepping closer and looking at the pad. A quizzical expression passed over her face. "I'll buy it from you anyway," she said, and then, "Oh dear. That didn't sound kind at all."

Millie laughed. "I hope I am not offended by the truth. Why would you want to purchase it?"

"I'm leaving this town, perhaps forever, and this is one of the things I would like to take with me in my mind and in my heart."

"Independence Hall?"

"The bell tower, really," the woman said. "And the bell in it."

"The bell is important to you?"

The woman nodded. "It has been there a very long time. It cracked the first time it was rung. They cast it new, but this time its voice was wrong, so they broke it, put it through the fire, and cast it again. Its voice was clear and true when it rang on July 8, 1776, to summon people to the first reading of the Declaration of Independence. But the crack is back. I've seen it myself. It's only a hairline now, but it will grow. It makes you wonder if bells have hearts as well as voices."

"How so?" Millie asked, truly curious now.

"There is an inscription on this bell you see," the woman answered. "It reads, 'Proclaim Liberty throughout all the land unto all the inhabitants thereof.' It is from Leviticus 25:10, where God describes the year of Jubilee, when all slaves were freed. How can this bell ring forth joyously when slavery exists in our land?"

"You are an abolitionist, then?" asked Millie.

"Yes," the woman replied.

"And a Quaker?" Millie flushed. "Pardon me. I have an inquisitive mind," she added.

"I am of the Society of Friends, yes," the young woman said, offering her hand. "My name is Angelina Grimke, and I believe every young woman should have an inquisitive mind."

CHAPTER

9

Speaking Up

*Speak up for those who cannot speak
for themselves, for the rights of
all who are destitute. Speak
up and judge fairly; defend
the rights of the poor
and needy.*

PROVERBS 31:8–9

Speaking Up

*T*he Angelina Grimke?" Millie asked. "Author of *Appeal to the Christian Women of the South*?"

"You've read it?" Angelina looked surprised, and then lowered her voice to a conspiratorial whisper. "It has made me notorious, I fear."

"I have practically memorized it! I . . . I can't believe it's you! This is remarkable!" said Millie, astonished. It took her a second to regain her composure, then she offered, "Won't you sit down?" As Millie moved her charcoal and bag to make room, she said, "My name is Millie Keith. I'm on my way to the South to stay with my uncle's family. I . . . I have some worries about how I will handle the situation."

Angelina glanced around nervously. The old gentleman had gone and the park was empty save for squirrels and pigeons. "You are from a free state, then?"

"Indiana. I was going to bring my copy of your book with me, but my father didn't think it would be wise," said Millie.

"Your father was correct." Angelina sighed and took a seat beside Millie. "I have become not only famous, but infamous because of that pamphlet. I can no longer even visit my home state of South Carolina, or my family in Charleston, without fear of imprisonment or worse."

"Imprisoned for writing a book?" asked Millie.

"I've never been to Indiana," Angelina said. "But even here in the city of brotherly love, abolitionist views have sparked violence. There were riots here last year, and the homes of some free blacks were destroyed. People who believe that the slaves should be freed are not always welcome. In fact, we are so unwelcome here that my sister and I are moving to New York City very shortly to work with the Anti-Slavery Society there. That's why I wanted the picture of the bell tower. To remember what this place stands for."

"I feel as if I am traveling into a great evil," Millie confessed. "And I have not had anyone to voice my fears to."

"Sometimes we have to look evil in the eye if we are going to change things." Angelina spoke as if she were seeing something far away, or perhaps remembering a distant past. "Many people in the free states have no idea what slavery is like. It is unimaginable to them that the stories the abolitionists publish could be true. They prefer to believe the fairy tales of happy slaves, singing and dancing in their servitude and being cared for like beloved children."

"The people of the North are guilty as well," Millie said. "The southern plantations feed the northern mills."

"Yes. The people of the North choose not to know, not to believe. The people of the South know, but choose not to change. Don't close your eyes, Millie Keith. Keep them open. Learn the truth, and you will have a chance someday to speak it."

"Your book was so clearly reasoned, and reasonably stated," Millie said. "I wish I could state the case for freedom half as well."

"Do you have a Bible?" asked Angelina.

"Yes," replied Millie.

"Everything you could possibly need is right in your Bible. Every word I wrote, every thought I expressed, had its origins there. And you know the Author of that Book never leaves you or forsakes you. Fill your heart with His words, and when you need them, they will spill out."

Millie nodded.

"There's something more, isn't there?" Angelina said. "You look very troubled."

"I have an aunt in Ohio and she cautioned me to be very careful who I spoke to, even among my relations. If everything my aunt told me is true . . . I'm afraid."

"You will be staying with an uncle?" Angelina asked. "What is his name?"

"Horace Dinsmore," said Millie.

Angelina frowned. "He married a young woman from Charleston, did he not?"

"Isabel Breandan," said Millie.

Angelina nodded. "Ah, yes, Isabel. We are close to the same age, and growing up in the same town I knew her well. The Dinsmores are a respectable family. But the Breandans . . . Millie, you must be careful. Mr. Breandan is the publisher of *The Morning Times* in Charleston. His family is wealthy, powerful and . . . cruel. Very cruel." Angelina closed her eyes for a moment, and Millie was sure she was praying. When she opened her eyes, Angelina went on. "I'm going to tell you something that you must not repeat, Millie Keith, because a time may come when you need to know it. But I must have your word that you won't ever speak of it."

Millie nodded and Angelina continued. "There are friends—even in the South. Watch for signs of the fishers of men—a fish, a net, a fishhook—on doors or in windows. These people can help you. But if you ever breathe a word about it, you will be putting their lives and the lives of many others in great danger."

A fishnet on the windowsill? thought Millie. "They are with the underground railroad, then?" she asked.

Millie's Remarkable Journey

"Let's just say they are willing to lay down their lives that others may be free," answered Angelina.

A fishnet on the windowsill! Millie didn't know whether to be relieved or even more worried than before. *Aunt Wealthy wasn't insane at all! She was hiding runaway slaves! No wonder she had been so distressed to see Uncle Horace!*

"Thank you," Millie said seriously. "You have helped me more than I can ever tell you! I want you to know that I am willing to lay down my life, too."

"Let's pray it doesn't come to that for you or for me, or any of our friends. But if it does . . . freedom must come to this nation, one way or another!"

Just then Arthur yelled from across the lawn, "Millie's talking to one of those peculiar people. Let's go see!"

"My cousins," Millie explained, as Miss Worth and the children arrived in a rush. Adelaide, Lora, and Louise were openly curious about Angelina's simple, unadorned clothes. Arthur and Walter examined her as they might an exhibit at the zoo. Miss Worth was reminding them of their manners when Uncle Horace arrived.

"How do you do?" he said, lifting his hat.

Angelina rose and offered her hand. "Horace Dinsmore. I doubt that you remember me, but I remember you. My name is Angelina Grimke. Your first wife was a dear friend of my sister Sarah."

"Sarah Grimke," Uncle Horace said. "Yes, she and Eva did have a great deal in common. How is your sister?"

"She is well. I will tell her you inquired after her. She is always pleased to hear from home. It was good talking to you, Millie. I must be on my way. I'm already late for my appointment, I'm afraid."

Speaking Up

"Wait!" exclaimed Millie. She tore the drawing of Independence Hall from her book and held it out. "I want you to have this."

"Thank you," said Angelina. She rolled it carefully to avoid smudging the charcoal. "I will treasure it," she said with a smile. "Goodbye."

Angelina started to cross the street, but a man met her halfway, stepping directly in front of her. His dress was that of a gentleman, but the look on his face was anything but gentlemanly. "Grimke!" He said it like a curse word, and spat. Only a sudden twirl of wind kept the spittle from staining Angelina's skirts.

"How rude!" Adelaide cried.

Uncle Horace was in the street in a flash, his silver-tipped cane at the man's throat like a rapier. "You *will* apologize."

Lora screamed. Millie pulled the little girl to her side with one arm and caught Walter, who had started after his father, by the collar with the other. "Shhh," Millie said. "Let your father take care of it." She glanced around to make sure Miss Worth had the other children in hand.

"Do you know who she is?" the man finally managed to squeak. "She's an abolitionist!"

"And you, sir, are a scoundrel who has insulted one of the daughters of Judge Grimke, a personal friend of mine. To say nothing of the fact that you have set a very bad example for my children." Uncle Horace's voice was calm, but the expression on his face was not. "You have one second to apologize before I thrash you."

The man's eyes moved to Angelina. "I . . . I apologize . . . ma'am."

"And humbly beg your pardon," Uncle Horace said, prompting a little with his cane.

Millie's Remarkable Journey

"And humbly beg your pardon," said the man. His eyes were locked on Uncle Horace now.

"You may go," Uncle Horace said.

The man fled, but whirled around after ten feet. "Dueling is illegal here!" he shouted. "I could summon the police!"

"Chastising dogs is not!" Uncle Horace replied. "And though I would never duel with the likes of you, sir, I will be happy to complete your education now." He took a step toward the street and the man fled.

"Thank you, Mr. Dinsmore!" Angelina said. "I have grown accustomed to being spat upon, cursed, and even struck with stones. But this is the first time I have been defended by a gentleman of the South!"

"I think you are wrong headed, madam," Uncle Horace said. "But I will not stand by while a coward insults a lady of Charleston. May I walk you to your appointment?"

"I must decline," Angelina said. "I am afraid you would not approve of the meeting I am on my way to attend. Goodbye, Mr. Dinsmore." She curtsied.

"Good day, Miss Grimke." He bowed.

They watched until Angelina disappeared around the corner, and then Uncle Horace turned and asked, "Now, what have my children been up to?"

"We got candy!" Walter said, pulling a peppermint stick from his pocket and offering it to his father. "I kept some for you." The little boy had apparently sampled the hard candy before putting it in his pocket. Uncle Horace pulled the lint and dust off before he popped it in his mouth. "Thank you, son," he said around the peppermint.

They continued their walk, Arthur and Walter now armed with sticks like their father's cane, stopping every

148

few yards to fence with bushes or trees. When they returned to the hotel, Isabel had risen at last and was awaiting them in the parlor. The children were spilling over with the news of the encounter.

"Father was in a duel!" Adelaide exclaimed. "He was terribly brave!"

"It was not a duel," Uncle Horace said. "It was nothing."

"It was something!" Arthur said. "A man spat at a lady named Grimke and Father threatened to thrash him!"

"Grimke! Why on earth would you defend that woman, Horace?" Isabel looked ready to spit herself. "You will repent of it the day we are found dead in our beds, our slaves having been driven to madness by her nonsense."

"Is someone going to kill us, Mother?" Walter asked.

"Not if we keep nasty people like the Grimkes away, darling," she said, petting his curls. "And if your father repents of defending them."

"I pray that defending a lady is all I have to repent of the day I am found dead," Uncle Horace said. "And I don't think you need to frighten the children with such talk."

The next day was the Sabbath. Isabel Dinsmore, though not religious, observed the social norms, attending church on Sundays. Uncle Horace, it seemed, was not regular in his attendance, but out of consideration for Millie and his wife, he agreed to go along. Millie was grateful for the chance to worship. The church was a stately brick building with a soaring steeple and huge wooden doors that swung out to welcome people into a quiet sanctuary. Millie had never seen a more beautiful church. The day had started off cloudy with a gusting wind, but the morning sun peeked through the clouds now, lancing through Peter's robe on the stained glass window and painting the dark wood of the altar as red as the Savior's blood.

The congregation was called to worship by the tones of a huge pipe organ. After the third hymn, a distinguished-looking man rose and walked to the pulpit.

"My friends," he said, "I want to present to you a pastoral letter that has been sent to every church in our city. In fact, this letter is being read from pulpits across this great nation. It addresses the dangers which at present seem to threaten the female character with widespread and permanent injury."

A murmur went through the crowd, and Mrs. Dinsmore snapped her fan open loudly, looking around as if the danger might be lurking in the shadows, ready to pounce on her daughters.

"I am speaking, of course, of the unnatural behavior of a certain lady of our city," the reverend continued, "a Miss Angelina Grimke." A shock went through Millie at the mention of the name. *Surely he could not mean the same gentle lady I spoke to yesterday—the writer of a book that calls for Christian women to look to the Bible, to their conscience, and to their Lord?*

The reverend began to read. The words of the letter were powerful and full of conviction, each line a condemnation of Angelina's behaviors and beliefs. "The appropriate duties and influence of women are clearly stated in the New Testament. She should be unobtrusive and private. . . . When she assumes the place and tone of man as public reformer, she yields the power which God has given her for protection!" At this, Mrs. Dinsmore cleared her throat loudly and looked at her husband. The reverend went on, "Her character becomes unnatural and she brings shame and dishonor on her name."

Angelina Grimke's own words from *Appeal to the Christian Women of the South* played counterpoint in Millie's brain: *"Are there no Shiprahs, no Puahs among you, who will dare in Christian firmness and Christian meekness, to refuse to obey the wicked laws which require woman to enslave, to degrade and to brutalize woman? Are there no Miriams, who would rejoice to lead out the captive daughters of the Southern States to liberty and light? Are there no Huldahs there who will dare to speak the truth concerning the sins of the people. . . ? Is there no Esther among you who will plead for the poor devoted slave?"*

Tears welled in Millie's eyes as she thought of these women of the Old Testament who were willing to follow the Lord despite great risk to themselves. The people seated in the pews around her were nodding their approval at the reverend's remarks, and Millie wanted to shout at them, or stand and leave. *But Mamma would never have done that,* Millie told herself. *Mamma would have said, "Jesus loves them, Millie. We need to love them too, and be gentle and prayerful and help them understand."*

The reverend finished the letter and proceeded to his sermon—a commentary on the text he had just read. When the sermon was done and the last hymn sung, the people filed out of the church one by one, shaking the reverend's hand on the way out and complimenting him on the power of his message.

I'm not going to say a word, Millie told herself as the line inched toward the door. *I am going to shake his hand and walk out. Nobody would listen to me anyway. I'm a stranger, and they would think me a child.*

Millie's Remarkable Journey

Isabel took the reverend's hand. "I am so thankful that we were here today," she said, giving her husband a look. "Some people need this message so much. I don't know what we would do without persons of authority warning us."

Millie bit her lip. *Not a word,* she promised herself.

"Thank you," the reverend said to Isabel. He turned and took Millie's hand, smiling warmly. "And what did you think of my message, young lady?"

"It was . . . it . . . I had some questions," Millie said. *So much for not saying a word! Lord, help me!*

"I specialize in answering questions," he said. "That's a reverend's job. Ask away."

"Have you ever met Angelina Grimke?" asked Millie.

"No," he laughed. "She's hardly the sort I would like to meet."

"Have you ever read any of her writings or heard her speak?" Millie realized her voice was shaking.

"Certainly not!" he said.

"Then how do you know that what you just read about her is true?" asked Millie respectfully.

"Why, everyone knows . . . "

"If everyone knows," she interrupted, "then why waste time preaching on it? Aren't sermons meant to instruct and convince?"

The reverend's smile froze. "You will understand these things when you are older," he said, turning to shake Uncle Horace's hand.

"She does have a point," Uncle Horace said seriously. "Good day, reverend."

The Dinsmores gathered silently on the walk to wait for their carriage. Millie realized that she had made a spectacle

of herself. Several people who had overheard the conversation pointed at her as they walked past. She suddenly wished that she were wearing her floppiest hat. She could pull it all the way down to her nose and pretend the world had disappeared.

"Have you read that woman's writings?" Isabel asked, looking at Millie with narrowed eyes.

"I have," Millie admitted.

"And what was your opinion of them?" asked Isabel.

"I . . ." Millie was saved by a commotion at the church door. The reverend pushed his way through the crowd and ran down the steps.

"There you are, young lady!" he said when he found Millie. "I would like to apologize for my behavior just now."

"There is no need," Millie began, but the reverend held up his hand.

"I do value the truth. And I have grown comfortable as the shepherd of this flock. Too comfortable, perhaps. Your questions were good ones. I can't believe I will ever agree with Angelina Grimke. But I agree with you that I should ask more questions. So thank you."

"Well, that is something I never thought I would see!" Uncle Horace said as they settled into the carriage. "Perhaps I should attend church more often."

Millie pulled baby Enna onto her lap to make more room on the seat for Adelaide. _Lord_, Millie prayed, _make me strong like the heroic women of the Bible. Give me the courage to do and to speak up for what is right in Your eyes — no matter what the risk to myself._

CHAPTER

10

An Outrage

Do not repay evil with evil or insult
with insult, but with blessing,
because to this you were called
so that you may inherit
a blessing.

1 PETER 3:9

An Outrage

*T*he next morning, Millie and the Dinsmore family boarded the ship that would take them to the port nearest to Roselands. After the trunks were delivered to their staterooms, Millie wrapped herself in Aunt Wealthy's red coat and a scarf and prepared to go on deck. The Dinsmores had a comfortable suite complete with a parlor, and Millie found her aunt, uncle, and cousins there.

"Preparing to go out?" Uncle Horace asked.

"Yes." Millie tucked the ends of her scarf into her jacket. "I was wondering if anyone would like to accompany me. I have never met the Atlantic. I think it would be lovely to make its acquaintance from the deck."

"I would be happy to go along. How about it, my dear?" Uncle Horace asked.

"Certainly not!" Isabel said. "Salt air is bad for the complexion."

"I want to go with Millie and Father," Adelaide said.

"Suit yourself," said Isabel, reclining on the couch. "I am sure you will be as pleasant-looking as a raisin by the time you are twenty! Bring me some tea, Jonati. And Miss Worth, *can* you keep Enna quiet? My head throbs!"

Millie found a comfortable spot by the rail. Adelaide stood between Millie and Uncle Horace, fascinated by the sights and sounds as the ship steamed down the river and out of the bay. Suddenly the horizon stretched blue and wide before them.

"Atlantic Ocean," Uncle Horace said formally, "I would like to present Miss Millie Keith. Millie, the Atlantic!" The

Millie's Remarkable Journey

Atlantic waved an aqua welcome, smacking the bow and sending a kiss of spray across their faces.

"A little forward for a first meeting!" Millie laughed, wiping her face.

"I think it likes you," Adelaide said, giggling.

"And I like it," replied Millie.

"Roselands is not so very far off from the coast," said Adelaide. "A ride of not too many miles from home brings us to a marvelous view."

"And we will place a pony and servant at your command, so that you can ride in that direction whenever you wish," added Uncle Horace.

Millie took her eyes from the sea long enough to thank him, but was immediately called back to it by a cry from Adelaide.

"Look, dolphins to bring us luck!" she said, pointing to two sleek creatures that arched out of the water in the wake of the boat.

"I will leave you two to the marvels of the ocean," Uncle Horace said. "I have a wife to attend to."

Millie and Adelaide kept to the deck all day, marveling over flights of pelicans and saucy seagulls fighting over scraps from the ship's galley. Finally the sun dipped under the land to the west, and the air turned so cold they were forced to seek the shelter of the cabin.

Isabel was still half reclining on the sofa, a damp cloth over her eyes. Uncle Horace sat by her side reading the evening paper. "I'm glad you've come in at last," Isabel said, sitting up. "I was certain my child had fallen overboard and been swept away!"

"If I had fallen in, Millie would have jumped in and saved me," Adelaide said with certainty.

"Don't be pert," Isabel admonished. "Ohhh, make the ship stop rocking, Horace! I will be deathly sick before morning."

"No one can hold back the waves, my dear. But you would be less likely to be sick if you followed Millie's example and stayed on deck," Uncle Horace said. "Perhaps tomorrow . . ."

"I will catch my death of cold, but no one would care! Will someone stop that noise!"

"Children!" Uncle Horace said. "Your mother needs quiet now."

Millie had a sudden longing for her own mother and father and brothers and sisters, and their home on Keith Hill. "May I tell the children a story, Aunt Isabel?" asked Millie.

"Anything to keep them quiet," said Isabel as she rubbed her brow.

Millie gathered the little ones around her on the opposite side of the cabin, and pulled Enna up on her lap. It somehow helped the ache to have a small person wrapped in her arms.

"Tell us a story about Indians," Arthur demanded. "Have you ever met an Indian?"

"Why, yes, I have," Millie said. Miss Worth came over and sat quietly in the background as Millie told the story of meeting members of the Potawatami tribe. The children listened and asked questions until they were interrupted by the summons to tea.

The sea was rough that night, causing a good deal of sickness among the passengers. Millie knew from past experience that lying in bed in the stuffy berth was no way to fight seasickness. She made her way to the deck as soon as the sky began to lighten. The sky was spangled with clouds this morning, and they announced the coming of the sun with ruffles of red and gold.

"How beautiful," whispered Adelaide, who had followed Millie onto the deck.

"It's creation shouting the glory of the Lord," Millie said seriously, "and His special blessing for everyone who got up early to talk with Him this morning!"

"Really?" Adelaide reached up as if she could touch a burning cloud. They stood together and watched as the sun crept over the horizon and then seemed to leap into the sky. "How beautiful," Adelaide said again.

"Haven't you ever seen the sun rise over the ocean? I would think you had, as you have traveled on ships before."

"I've never seen the sunrise before," Adelaide said seriously. "Mother doesn't approve of waking early."

Millie was joined by all of her cousins and their nursemaid after breakfast. Uncle Horace was caring for Isabel. Millie and Miss Worth kept the children on deck as much as possible for the rest of the voyage. When the vessel arrived in port, Isabel emerged from her stateroom leaning on her husband's arm. She improved amazingly as soon as her foot touched solid ground.

Once ashore, Millie looked around curiously. She was standing on the soil of a slave state. There were black workers along the docks—more black faces than white, in fact. The slaves were not dressed as well as the personal servants she had seen traveling with their masters. The men wore loose cotton britches, and many wore no shirt. The women Millie could see in the distance wore colorful skirts and shirts, and kerchiefs on their heads. Ladies and gentlemen smiled and nodded greetings to

An Outrage

Isabel and Uncle Horace, glancing at Millie. She tried not to return their stares.

Two coaches from Roselands were waiting, and Uncle Horace helped Millie, Isabel, and the older girls into the first, and the rest of the children, Miss Worth, and Jonati into the second. Millie was glad to have the seat nearest the window. The small seaport was quaint and lovely, with red brick storefronts and homes.

"Horace, I think I will have a party on Friday of next week," said Isabel, whose miraculous recovery was now complete. "We have an obligation to present Millie, and I'm sure I can't do it sooner, and if we do it later, the neighbors will think there is something wrong with her."

"A party is a wonderful idea," Uncle Horace said.

"Then we shall have to stop at Mrs. Bissell's today and have Millie measured. My seamstresses will be quite busy with my gown, so she will have to hire her own. As soon as word of the party leaks out, Mrs. Bissell will be too busy to take on any new clients."

"Mrs. Bissell is very good," Uncle Horace assured Millie, winking. "I'm sure you will want to hire her services. We can order the fabrics to be left here, and return for the dresses."

"Driver!" Uncle Horace called to the coachman. "We will be stopping at the dressmaker's." Poor Jonati and Miss Worth were left sitting in the second coach with the children as Isabel led Millie toward the dressmaker's shop.

Millie was amused to see that the shop next door was Blessed Bliss's Funeral Parlor. "We grieve for you!" the sign announced. A thin gentleman with a morose face was cleaning the windows. He could only be Mr. Bliss, Millie decided. She could imagine Dearest by his side weeping quietly at their wedding. Millie hoped she would be able to visit her new friends when they returned from their trip.

"I'll leave you two ladies to your business," Uncle Horace said, walking back to the other coach to talk to the children while they waited.

Isabel led Millie into the dressmaker's shop. It was fascinating. There were headless women's forms wearing dresses in various stages of completion, and small closets full of fabrics, ribbons, buttons, and bows along each wall. They were greeted by a plain but friendly woman. Millie's measurements were taken, and the fabric and dresses discussed. Millie was instructed to choose lace and ribbon from one of the closets while Isabel gave instructions to Mrs. Bissell for a gown of her own, which she had apparently been inspired to order while discussing Millie's party dress.

Millie was feeling the texture of a red velvet ribbon when Isabel gasped. "Oh, good heavens, not Mrs. Landreth!"

Before Millie could turn around, she found herself shoved into a tiny closet and the door shut behind her. Her nose was pressed against a drawer of buttons, and something sharp poked her hip.

"Be *perfectly* quiet," Isabel hissed, and then, in a most pleasant tone, "Mrs. Landreth! And Charles, how are you?"

What on earth? Millie squirmed, trying to make room in the dark cramped space. *Certainly Isabel does not approve of my dress, but going to this extreme to keep me out of sight? It's ridiculous!* Millie pushed against the door, but it was latched. *Should I start shouting?*

"Mrs. Dinsmore," a sour voice replied. "I thought you were away."

An Outrage

"We have returned," Isabel said brightly. "The Dinsmores are back, and there will be a ball at Roselands in one week! You will receive an invitation of course, Charles."

A deep voice answered, but Millie could not make out the words. The pin bit at her side, and she tried to wiggle away from it with no success.

"Are you here to order a dress?" Isabel asked.

"Just to pick up a parcel," Mrs. Landreth said. "Charles has come along to carry it."

Millie heard a rustling, goodbyes, and a door shutting, and then Isabel pulled the closet door open.

"You're welcome!" she said.

"You expect me to thank you for locking me in a closet?" Millie was furious. "I'm sorry, but I did not find it pleasant!"

"It was for your own good. That," said Isabel, indicating a pair of wide shoulders disappearing down the street, "was Charles Landreth, the most eligible gentleman in the area. His fortune is quite large, and his family of the first cloth. He would be an excellent catch for you. Naturally I assumed that you would not want to meet him looking like," her eyes went over Millie from toes to hat, "*that.*"

"I do not want to meet him at all," Millie said. "And I will thank you not to shove me into any more closets!" She stomped out of the shop. Isabel followed.

Uncle Horace looked from Isabel to Millie when they returned to the street.

"Is everything all right?" he asked.

"No, it is not," Isabel said. "Your niece has no sense."

"What is this all about?" he asked, helping Millie into the stagecoach.

Millie's Remarkable Journey

"Charles Landreth," Millie said, flinging herself into the corner. "Ouch!" she had apparently carried the straight pin in her skirt. She pulled it out. "I will keep this to remember Mr. Landreth by!"

"May I ask . . . " Uncle Horace began.

"No!" Isabel said.

"I see." Uncle Horace settled in, and the stagecoach was on its way.

Millie rode in silence for a few moments. *She's horrible! She should know better than . . . she should know better!* Millie glanced at her aunt's profile. Was it possible that the woman really was trying to keep her from embarrassment? She had made a spectacle of herself in front of Mrs. Bissell. *Lord*, Millie prayed, *help me not to be so hotheaded. If it is even remotely possible that she was thinking of me rather than herself, shouldn't I give her a chance?*

"Aunt Isabel?" said Millie.

Isabel sniffed, which Millie took as a reply.

"I apologize for getting angry. I do believe you had my best interests at heart, but being shoved suddenly into a closet was unsettling. And I truly have no desire for a romance," said Millie.

"You must learn to respect your elders," Isabel said. The ice in her voice was perhaps a little less thick. "It's going to be a lovely party."

Roselands was a good distance inland. The land between the small town and the plantation was mostly fields. Millie had never seen a cotton plant before, but she recognized the low shrub-like greenery by the white puffs of cotton bursting from the bolls. The sun was sinking, but far from the road Millie could see a line of men, women, and children with sacks on their backs, apparently picking cotton.

An Outrage

"Do these fields belong to Roselands?" Millie asked.

"Yes," Uncle Horace said proudly. "You have been on Dinsmore land almost since we left town, and all of it in cotton. We require over three hundred field hands, and borrow more from Isabel's family during harvest. We are almost through harvest now, and my manager writes that it has been an excellent year."

They reached Roselands just as the sun was setting amid a mass of crimson, gold, and amber-colored clouds forming a landscape so beautiful it took Millie's breath away.

"Roselands has that effect on people," Isabel said with satisfaction.

"Let me bid you welcome and hope that first impressions may prove lasting, and your stay here most enjoyable," Uncle Horace said with a smile. No one bothered with their bags or trunks—slaves were already attending to those. The family walked up the wide steps together.

A dozen or more house slaves, led by the housekeeper, a very respectable-looking white woman, stood in a double row across the veranda and down the wide entrance hall. They were smiling, their hands held out in greeting, with glad words of welcome on every tongue, as master, mistress, guest, and children, with their attendants, passed slowly between the ranks. Their seeming delight at Mrs. Dinsmore's return gave Millie some hope that Isabel's cross behavior was due to dislike of travel.

CHAPTER

11

Royal Treatment

*Be wise in the way you act
toward outsiders; make
the most of every
opportunity.*

COLOSSIANS 4:5

"rs. Brown, this young lady is my niece Millie Keith from the state of Indiana," said Uncle Horace, laying a hand on Millie's shoulder and addressing himself to the housekeeper. "I commend her to your special care. Please see that she is well waited upon, and wants for nothing that house or plantation can supply."

"Yes, sir," replied Mrs. Brown, a kind-looking lady with a rosy complexion and reassuring blue eyes. "Welcome to Roselands, Miss Keith."

Millie started to speak, but was interrupted by Isabel's calling out, "Here, Laylie!"

A young, sun-bronzed girl of perhaps ten years old appeared suddenly. Millie looked at her uncle in surprise. *Surely he's told Aunt Isabel how I feel about slaves and she's assigned me a hired servant instead of a slave.*

"I appoint you Miss Millie's waiting maid, Laylie," said Isabel. "You are to be always at her call, and do whatever she directs."

"Yes, mistress," the girl answered, dropping a deep curtsey. "Shall I show the way to your room now, miss?" she asked Millie.

"Please," replied Millie. She was led to a spacious, elegantly furnished apartment. The walls were paneled in light oak, and an open wood fire blazed and crackled, giving the room a ruddy light that made the glow of the candles on the mantel unnecessary.

"This is a lovely room," Millie said to the girl. "Laylie? Was that your name?"

The girl turned wide, curious eyes to her. "Yes, miss."

"Do you think there is time to dress before tea?" Millie asked.

The girl considered a moment and then nodded. "Plenty of time."

Two men entered with Millie's luggage. Mrs. Brown followed close in their rear, bade them unstrap Millie's trunk before leaving, inquired of Millie if there was anything more she could do for her, and said she hoped Millie would be very comfortable. "Laylie is young and has not had much experience in the duties of lady's maid," she said, casting a worried look at the girl, "though I hope you will find her trustworthy and willing. Would you like to have her unpack your things and arrange them in the bureau and wardrobe? Then the trunk can be put away out of sight till it's wanted again."

"I could use some help," said Millie, producing the keys. "But I doubt we will finish before tea."

"What does that matter?" Mrs. Brown said with a laugh. "Laylie will finish while you eat. You do it exactly as I showed you now, Laylie."

As Mrs. Brown took her departure, Uncle Horace looked in for a moment to see that his young guest had not been neglected, and to make sure she was pleased with her new quarters.

When Millie turned back to her trunk at last, Laylie was pulling out her dresses, examining each new find as it emerged from the trunk. She seemed more intent on emptying the trunk than bringing order to the wardrobe. Millie smiled. *She's helping just like Fan would at home—by making a mess.*

"Laylie, you don't have to unpack for me," Millie said, rescuing a dress from her and laying it on the bed. "You go

ahead and have your tea too, and we'll finish before bedtime."

"We don't have tea, miss. We won't have supper until the work is done, after the white folks are gone to bed. Let me help you with that dress, miss."

White folks? Isabel didn't assign me a hired servant at all! Millie realized with a shock. Millie looked at the young girl again. *She looks as if she could be one of Rhoda Jane Lightcap's little sisters. She has the same wide brown eyes, brown braids, and dark, suntanned skin. But Laylie must be a mulatto.*

"I am good at dressing myself," Millie said with a smile. "It's something one learns on the frontier." She pulled off her travel outfit, grabbed the new dress from the bed, and slipped it over her head. She buttoned it quickly and then pulled a brush from her bag and ran it through her hair. Just moments later, the tea bell rang and Miss Worth, the children's governess, peeked in the door.

"If you are ready, Miss Keith, I'll show you the way," she said. Then, noticing the young girl, she stepped into the room and asked, "Laylie, what's wrong? What is going on here?" The little girl was standing with her arms folded across her chest and her lips pressed together in an angry expression. "She won't let me *do* anything," Laylie said, clearly irritated.

"Then you stand and do nothing until you are given permission to speak," Miss Worth said firmly. "You don't want to visit Mrs. Dinsmore, do you?" she asked, eyebrows raised.

Laylie dropped her eyes. "No, miss."

"And I am very sure Mrs. Brown told you to unpack this trunk."

"Yes, miss," said Laylie.

Millie's Remarkable Journey

Millie and Miss Worth stepped into the hall. Miss Worth looked both ways to make sure they were alone, then said, "I think you are a good person, Miss Keith. But you are a stranger here and this is a strange land—one you don't understand."

"I . . . I didn't realize Laylie was a . . . is she a mul . . . " Millie flushed, realizing the indelicacy of her question. "Pardon me, Miss Worth. Don't feel you need to answer."

"I know what you are asking," Miss Worth said. "And the answer is yes. Laylie is a mulatto. Laylie was sent up with a group of field slaves on loan from Meadshead, the Breandan's plantation, the week before we left. The harvest is later in Charleston, and we will send slaves to them to help as soon as the harvest here is done. If Laylie does well, Mrs. Dinsmore may allow her to stay here as a house slave. If she doesn't, she will be sent to the fields."

"Doesn't she want to return to her parents?" asked Millie.

"Her mother is dead," Miss Worth said shortly.

"And her father?"

Miss Worth did not reply, and Millie flushed again.

"I want to thank you, Miss Worth. There are a great many things I do not know, and a great many mistakes I will make. I would appreciate your help and friendship while I am here."

"This is Mrs. Dinsmore's idea of a joke," Miss Worth said. "Laylie is just out of the slave children's house, you see, and has no training at all. Mrs. Dinsmore prides herself on breaking in domestics." She stopped and looked at Millie. "I can't presume to tell you what to do. But if you let Laylie serve you, and help her learn what is expected of her, you will save her a great deal of pain."

172

"I will do what I can, Miss Worth," said Millie.

They entered the dining room and Miss Worth took her place at the table. Uncle Horace showed Millie to the seat of honor at his right hand, and complimented her on the becomingness of her dress.

"We don't always get to dine with Father and Mother," Adelaide whispered. "Only when there are no guests."

The table was loaded with delicacies, skillfully prepared. The cloth was snowy damask, the plates fine china, and the silverware heavy and old. Millie was amazed that the Dinsmore children handled their plates and glasses so carefully, though Jonati, who was standing in the background, cut the smaller children's food into bite-sized pieces before they began.

"This bread is wonderful," Millie said.

"Our cook, Phoebe, is a genius in the culinary arts," Isabel said. "I can't tell you how many people have tried to buy her from me. But you don't part with family heirlooms. My grandfather purchased her mother straight off the block from Africa. Phoebe has never been near a slave auction, though I could get more for her than for a healthy male field hand, I'm sure. My father knew his slaves and he bred for quality, pure quality."

The food on Millie's plate seemed suddenly less appealing.

"Let's not discuss business at the table, dear," Uncle Horace said.

They finished the meal making small talk about the weather and news of their neighbors. "I am so exhausted," Isabel said when the meal was over. "I'm sure I can't stay awake another moment." She rose and, to Millie's surprise, kissed Uncle Horace on the cheek, saying, "It is good to be home." Then Isabel took her leave, and Jonati ushered the children out of the room.

Millie's Remarkable Journey

"Are you thinking of bed too, or would you like to see the library?" Uncle Horace asked Millie.

"A library!" she cried. "How could I sleep knowing I hadn't seen it?"

"I thought you would feel that way," said Uncle Horace, smiling.

He led Millie down several hallways to a huge room. The fire in the grill was burning low, the light barely reaching the walls. It took Millie a moment to realize that the shelves reached from carpet to ceiling along three walls. Each shelf was neatly filled with books. "I didn't know there were so many books in the world!" Millie said.

"Some of them are quite old," Uncle Horace said. "Roselands has few neighbors. As a boy I came to this room looking for friends, and I found many. Here I can converse with the great thinkers of time." He stoked the fire as he spoke and the flames leapt up, illuminating the room. The floor was plush with Turkish carpet and smaller, handsome rugs. There were several large chairs and couches, and tables beside them covered with books, papers, and periodicals.

"This is my sanctuary," Uncle Horace explained. "A place completely apart from the rest of the world. Horace Jr. was fond of it, but none of the others have discovered its attractions yet. Perhaps they will in time."

Millie sank into a comfortable chair and looked around her in amazement. This collection of books made Aunt Wealthy's library look shabby, and Aunt Wealthy had a very fine collection indeed.

"I want you to feel perfectly at home here," Uncle Horace said. "Help yourself to books and writing materials, for whatever is in the room is entirely at your service."

Royal Treatment

"Thank you! May I take a book to my room?" she asked.

"As many as you like. But I thought you would rather attend to these first." He held out a bundle of mail.

"Letters from home! I have been so starved for them, Uncle!"

Millie took the letters and sorted them on her lap. Mamma and Pappa had written, of course, and her sister Zillah, Rhoda Jane Lightcap, and Reverend and Mrs. Lord had written, too.

"If you would like to read them here, I will be no bother," Uncle Horace said. "I would like news of the family, if there is any you care to share."

Millie nodded and moved to a chair closer to the fire, holding her mother's letter to the light. Voices from home seemed to fill the room as she read. There was news about the girls' progress in school and the planning of the Christmas Social, and her mother inquired about Aunt Wealthy's health.

"Here's news for you, Uncle," Millie said, reading aloud from Zillah's letter: " 'Don and Cyril could not decide on a name for the pup. Pappa said that it did not matter what they named him officially, they could always call him "Bob" for short, because of his poor tail. They were still fighting over a name when Nicholas Ransquate came to show them his new hat.' "

"A new hat?" said Millie, looking up from her reading. "Who could Nicholas possibly be buying a hat for? Have I forgotten a birthday, or is there someone new in town?"

"For himself, I assume," Uncle Horace said. "As you just mentioned, it was his hat."

"Yes, of course," Millie said, realizing her uncle had no idea of the significance of a hat perched on Nicholas's head.

She went back to the letter: " ' "What do you call your dog?" Mr. Ransquate asked. "Bob for short," Don said. "But what is his full name?" asked Nicholas. "What?" Cyril said, holding up the poor tail. "Ain't Bobforshort long enough for you?" And so the pup's name is and will remain Bobforshort.' "

"An amusing word play," Uncle Horace said, his face softening as it did when he thought about laughing. *He did spend a lot of time alone here as a child*, Millie decided. *Too much time.*

The rest of the letters were full of the doings of friends and family. Rhoda Jane wrote that Damaris's act of charity seemed to have changed her life. She had apparently given Millie all of her good clothes to travel in, and so had to sew more for herself. Amazingly, she had chosen not the dull, somber colors of her past, but newer colors, styles, and fashions.

"It is astounding," Rhoda Jane wrote, "what an improvement a new wardrobe can make!" The voices stilled as Millie laid the last letter down and wiped a tear from her cheek. She hadn't even realized she was crying.

Uncle Horace cleared his throat uncomfortably. "I think we must have a ride tomorrow morning, you and Adelaide and myself. Would you like that?"

"Very much," Millie said.

"Shall we say eleven o'clock?"

"Eleven? That's practically afternoon, Uncle! Though I could go riding at any time of day or night."

He considered a moment.

"I had forgotten your frontier ways. Surely you won't rise with the sun tomorrow? Allow yourself to sleep in. I know Adelaide will," he said. "Let's have our ride directly

after breakfast, which will not be earlier than nine. Now I see you are wanting to retire, so goodnight."

Millie returned to her room, which was as bright, warm, and cheery as she had left it. Laylie was not there, and the trunk had vanished also. Millie opened the wardrobe to find her clothes neatly hung. The bureau drawers were also full.

Aunt Wealthy's ointment was on her dressing table. Millie had just finished applying it and was replacing the lid when Laylie came back in to replenish the fire.

"Is there anything you need, miss? Hot chocolate or toast?"

"No, thank you. My needs are fully supplied," Millie said, smiling.

"I wasn't sure where to put that," Laylie said, indicating the ointment. "Is it perfume, miss?"

"No," Millie said with a smile. "It's my Aunt Wealthy's miracle cure. Good for coughs, cuts, and burns," Millie said, imitating her aunt's voice. "I put it on before I get ready for bed."

"You are getting ready for bed? Then you must want your slippers and night clothes, miss," said Laylie, hastening to bring them. "Shall I brush out your hair?"

Millie started to decline the offer, but remembering Miss Worth's advice, changed her mind.

"Yes, when I have put on my dressing gown. I'll read while you are brushing."

Millie put on her gown and sat at the dressing table with her Bible in front of her. Laylie began to brush Millie's hair, and, to Millie's relief, Laylie was much gentler than Jonati had been. Millie glanced at the girl's reflection in the mirror. Her hands were busy with the brush, but her eyes were on the book lying open on the dressing table. The look on Laylie's face could only be described as yearning.

"Do you read, Laylie?" asked Millie.

The girl jumped. "No, miss! That's for white folks. We're not allowed."

Of course, Millie thought. *I knew that. Slaves are not allowed to learn to read.* Millie thought of the library downstairs—a banquet of books waiting to be opened, words waiting to be read. And here was a child whose eyes were hungry for words.

"I read my Bible every night before I go to sleep," Millie explained.

"What's a Bible?" asked Laylie. "Is it a book?"

"You have never heard of the Bible?" asked Millie, amazed.

"I've lived all my life at Meadshead Plantation. Black folk don't have books there. I've seen them, though, in the big house."

How can I explain the Bible? It is certainly much more than a book. "The Bible is a little bit like a letter," Millie said, thinking how wonderful it was to receive letters from her family who knew her and cared about her. "It's like a letter from Jesus to us. To me and to you. It's full of His thoughts, His plans, and the things He wants us to do."

"Is this Jesus a mister or a missus?" asked Laylie.

"A Mister," said Millie.

"Well, somebody ought to tell him that you can get into big trouble for writing letters to black people. We're not allowed to have them."

She's never heard of Jesus! Millie realized in surprise. Millie knew that some plantation owners encouraged their slaves to be Christians, even providing church services for them.

But others forbade it, thinking the slaves would view themselves as the suffering Israelites in Egypt, longing for freedom. *Is it possible that a child could grow to ten years of age in such isolation that she truly doesn't know what a Bible is? That she has never heard the name of Jesus?*

"Can you listen, if someone else reads?" Millie asked.

The girl looked thoughtful. "Nobody said I can't," she decided at last. "I guess that means I can."

"Then I'll read the Bible to you every night and morning while you do my hair," Millie said. She opened to the book of Genesis.

"In the beginning, God created the heavens and the earth." Millie read slowly, pointing to each word as she spoke it, just as she'd done with Fan when she was learning to read. Millie glanced up once, checking the reflection in the mirror. Laylie's eyes were on the page, following along closely.

CHAPTER

12

The Key

Teach me, and I will be quiet;
show me where I have
been wrong.

JOB 6:24

The Key

There was a crackling fire on the hearth when Millie woke the next morning. Laylie was sitting cross-legged before it, poking the flames with a stick. Millie watched the little girl for a moment, wondering what she dreamed as she watched the orange flames. Zillah dreamed of getting married and having a family of her own in Pleasant Plains. Adah wanted to move to New York City and work with poor people the way Aunt Wealthy did when she was young. Mamma said dreams were seeds that God planted in a child's heart, seeds that were precious to Him. *I wonder what dreams God has planted in Laylie's heart.*

The little girl looked up suddenly, realizing Millie was awake, and jumped to her feet. "Good morning, miss."

"Good morning, Laylie," Millie said, stretching. "Have you had breakfast already?"

"Yes, miss."

"I wish I had," Millie said. "I understand that breakfast is not served until nine."

"Should I fetch you toast and tea?"

"No, thank you," Millie said. "I will read my Bible and then write some letters. By that time surely they will be serving breakfast."

Millie got up and walked across the room to open the drapes, but Laylie rushed ahead and opened them. Then Millie took a seat at the dressing table and opened her Bible. She read the second chapter of Genesis aloud slowly as Laylie brushed her hair. Once again, when Millie glanced in the mirror, she could see the little girl's eyes following her finger across the page. Millie kept reading until her hair was braided and tied with ribbons.

"Thank you," Millie said when Laylie finished, at a loss to think of what the little girl should do next. *What are the responsibilities of a personal servant?* She needed time to think, pray, and ask questions of Miss Worth. "I think I'll go to the library now to write my letters," Millie decided. "After breakfast, I will go for a ride with Uncle Horace and Adelaide." Laylie nodded.

Millie allowed Laylie to help her dress, then gathered up her writing supplies and Bible. She started to leave, but turned back at the door. *How many halls did I walk down last night? How many turns to the right or left?* She was not sure she could find the dining room, much less the library. "Laylie, do you know where the library is?" Millie asked. "I'm not sure I can find my way."

The little girl led her down the stairs and through the halls to the library door, where she stopped. "We don't go in this room," Laylie said, standing on tiptoe to peek in over Millie's shoulder.

Millie was relieved to find the library empty, and quickly settled into her writing. She penned a note to Rhoda Jane describing the characters at Blessed Bliss's funeral home, to her sisters describing the hat shop in Philadelphia, and to her brothers telling of the train ride and combustible bustle.

She spent more time and thought over the letter to her parents. She longed to tell her mother about meeting Angelina Grimke, but after some thought left it out. If Angelina and Aunt Wealthy were correct, it might not be wise to put it down in ink. She could tell her mother all about it when she arrived home in just three months.

The Key

What can I tell Mamma about Laylie? Millie wondered. She wanted to ask her Mamma's advice, but instead described the beauty of Roselands and the lovely dresses she was having made. "I am having a wonderful time, and my lungs seem much stronger. My cough is hardly a problem now, except at night. I know you pray for me, Mamma, and I pray for you, too, and everyone in Pleasant Plains. I miss you so much. Love, Millie." She folded the letter and sighed deeply as she put it in her pocket.

Of course I should tell Laylie about Jesus . . . shouldn't I? If she cannot read the Bible, how can she learn about Jesus after I'm gone? No one here is going to teach her. Teaching slaves to read is against the law. Dear Jesus, I asked You to help me be like the heroic women of the Bible, but all they had to be was brave. They weren't breaking any laws, were they?

Millie knew without asking what Uncle Horace would think about teaching a slave to read. He would be hurt and disappointed that she had abused his hospitality in such a way. Millie wished she could talk to her Mamma or Aunt Wealthy for just one moment. This was the hardest decision she had ever had to make, and she felt alone. *But I'm not alone,* she told herself. *God promised He would never leave me or forsake me. So what do you think, Lord? What should I do? You said in the book of James that anyone who lacks wisdom can ask You for it and You will grant it generously. So I'm asking You, Lord. Please grant me Your wisdom!* Millie hugged her Bible. The answer had to be there. There had to be someone in the Bible who faced this kind of a choice, someone to lead the way. *Help me, Lord,* Millie prayed.

As she sat there thinking, the names Shiphrah and Puah came into her mind. Millie knew they were Hebrew midwives in Egypt. Other than in Angelina Grimke's writings, she hadn't read about them for a long time, so she opened her Bible and searched until she found their story in the first chapter of Exodus. She read aloud, "The king of Egypt said to the Hebrew midwives, whose names were Shiphrah and Puah, 'When you help the Hebrew women in child-birth and observe them on the delivery stool, if it is a boy, kill him; but if it is a girl, let her live.'" *Certainly if the king ordered it, it was the law,* Millie reasoned. Then she continued: "'The midwives, however, feared God and did not do what the king of Egypt had told them to do; they let the boys live.'" Millie read the rest of the story and then considered it in silence. *It says that God was pleased with Shiphrah and Puah and blessed them for what they did. But that was a matter of life and death. This is just . . . just about reading the Bible.*

Millie bit her lip as she reflected further on the story. *A midwife helps babies be born into the world. Isn't a Christian supposed to help them be born into God's Kingdom?* Millie sensed somehow that there was an answer there for her, so she prayed again, "Lord, grant me Your wisdom."

If a midwife helped a baby be born and then left it alone without warmth or milk, wouldn't it die? Of course it would! But isn't the Bible the spiritual milk a baby Christian needs to grow? she reasoned. *Of course it is, because faith in Jesus is the only way to eternal life!*

"So this is a matter of life and death!" Millie exclaimed out loud. Suddenly all question was gone from Millie's mind. God *had* written the Bible for Laylie, too. Of course God wanted her to know Him and his Son, Jesus Christ! Any law that forbade Laylie to learn about Jesus was wrong, just as the Egyptian king had been wrong when he ordered the baby boys killed. Millie decided she was going to tell Laylie about Jesus. And she was going to teach the little girl to read.

The Key

Thank You, Lord, for preparing me by allowing me to teach my brothers and sisters. Help me do my job well! She was still praying when the bell rang to summon the Dinsmores to breakfast.

"And what have you been doing up so early?" Isabel asked. "I'm sure it's not good for you. You have shadows under your eyes."

"Not at all, Aunt Isabel," Millie said with a smile. "I am used to rising very early."

Isabel raised her teacup and considered Millie over the rim as she took a sip. "And how is the girl working out for you?"

"Laylie?" Millie said. "I think we will get along well. I do have a question for you, though. I have several letters to send to my family and friends. How do I post them?"

"I take care of all the posts," Isabel said. "Just give them to me after breakfast."

Millie was suddenly very thankful she had said nothing about Laylie or Angelina Grimke in her letters.

By the time they finished breakfast the horses were ready at the door. Dolly, the black mare Uncle Horace had chosen for Millie, had white stockings and a sweet blaze on her face. Millie gave Dolly a horehound candy she had taken from the bowl on the table and petted her nose before allowing Uncle Horace to lift her into the saddle. Adelaide's pony, Gypsy, was fat from lack of exercise, as her mistress had been gone some weeks. "Its just like sitting on a barrel, Father," Adelaide complained. "I feel as if I will roll off!"

"Poor Gypsy needs more exercise," Uncle Horace said. "But I'm afraid the groom is far too large to ride her." Uncle Horace's sorrel gelding, however, was in beautiful shape, obviously the pet of the groom.

Millie's Remarkable Journey

The three of them rode at a brisk canter for fifteen minutes, until Gypsy was puffing in her effort to keep up with the larger horses. Then they walked for a long time, leaving the well-developed roads and climbing a rolling hill that ultimately led them to a spot from which they could see the ocean in the distance. It was a calm day, and waves could be seen rolling placidly toward the shore.

"This was one of your mother's favorite spots when she came to visit many, many years ago," Uncle Horace said. "She loved to sit and read under that tree."

"It's beautiful, Uncle. I would like to come sketch here."

Their ride back was just as pleasant. Uncle Horace lifted first Adelaide and then Millie down from their saddles, and the groom led the horses away. It was a strange and pleasant experience for Millie. At home when she wanted to ride, she saddled Glory herself and mounted by climbing up on a fence rail in the yard. When her ride was over, she took the saddle and bridle off, and rubbed Glory down.

"You may ride every day if you wish," Uncle Horace said, "though I'm afraid Adelaide will have to be in the classroom. I hear that she neglected her studies while we were traveling." Adelaide groaned.

Isabel was already hard at work planning the party. Invitations were sent by messenger that afternoon, and cards from people who would be delighted to attend began trickling back that evening. Isabel checked the pile and sighed.

"Are you looking for a card from someone in particular, dear?" Uncle Horace asked. "You know everyone will attend. Your parties are legendary."

The next day was the Sabbath, but Isabel declared herself too tired to attend church and insisted that the children should also have a day of rest. Millie had to content herself

with a prayer walk around the garden. When Isabel realized that Millie was preparing for a walk, she asked if the children might go along. It was Miss Worth's afternoon off and Jonati had her hands full with the baby. Millie was happy to agree. She had not had much time to spend alone with her cousins, as they were always in the charge of their governess or nanny.

By the middle of the afternoon, Millie was certain that Adelaide and Walter were her favorites. They were serious and thoughtful like their father. Arthur, on the other hand, enjoyed throwing stones at squirrels and birds, and teasing his sisters. Millie was sure he crushed a baby field mouse under his boot just to make Lora cry, but the boy denied it, saying it was an accident. Millie found herself comparing him to Cyril and Don, and none too favorably, either. If Cyril were here, she was sure Arthur would soon be sporting a black eye, and he would learn quickly enough not to pick on creatures smaller than himself.

Louise and Lora were very like their mother in disposition. They did not enjoy walking in the garden, as the grass might stain their shoes, and they did not enjoy sitting in the porch swing, as the November shade was a little too cool. Millie was heartily glad when the afternoon was over and she was able to return to her own thoughts in her own room. She had tried to talk to Laylie, but could not find a time or place in the big house where they might not be disturbed. Maids or the housekeeper came in at all times, and Isabel had questions about the party and Millie's taste in food. It was clear to Millie that for any serious talking to occur, they would have to be somewhere more private.

On Monday morning the children had breakfast and retired to the classroom with Miss Worth. Isabel was fully occupied planning the party. Millie found her Uncle Horace in the library catching up with the duties of running the plantation.

"The northern factories are bleeding us dry," Uncle Horace said, putting down his pen in disgust. "They buy our cotton at rock bottom prices, then turn around and sell us everything we need to produce it, from shoes for our slaves to machinery, at top dollar. But you didn't come to discuss business, I hope."

"No," Millie said. "I would like to take my sketchbook out to the bluff we visited to do some drawing. I was wondering if we might accomplish two things at once."

"Two things?"

"Well, I would like some company, and Gypsy would like some exercise. May I take Laylie along with me until Adelaide is fully caught up with her work?"

"I don't see why not," Uncle Horace said. "I'll order the horses brought for you. When would you like to go? After breakfast tomorrow, perhaps?"

"Thank you, Uncle. That would be wonderful," replied Millie.

"I hope you don't think it is this quiet at Roselands all of the time," he said with a smile. "Isabel is only waiting for your dresses to be done, and the parties will begin. After that, Millie, you may never want to go home."

"I doubt that, Uncle. You are very kind, but I do miss my family."

That night after Millie read her Bible, she set it aside and asked, "Laylie, would you like to ride with me tomorrow?"

"On a horse?" The little girl looked surprised, but delighted.

"Do you know how to ride a horse?" Millie asked.

"No, miss, but I hold on good."

The next morning after breakfast, Dolly and Gypsy were waiting at the steps. Uncle Horace had apparently taken Millie's art supplies into consideration, as Dolly wore saddlebags. Millie put her sketchbook and charcoal in one and her Bible in the other. The groom said nothing as he lifted Laylie up into the saddle and handed her the reins. The little girl gripped them in one hand and wrapped the other hand in Gypsy's mane.

"Now, do just what I do," Millie said. She turned her mare and started walking her up the drive. Laylie sat straight and tall on Gypsy's back, imitating Millie's every move. The fat pony followed along with no prompting from Laylie at all. Millie walked the mare in the direction of the bluff. Fat little Gypsy kept her nose on the trail behind Dolly the whole way. Eventually, Millie dismounted, making sure there was a rock nearby big enough to allow her to mount again. She tied Dolly's reins and then reached up to help Laylie down.

"Well?" Millie asked. "Do you like riding?"

"Yes, miss."

"I'm going to draw for a little while," Millie said. She took her paper, charcoal, and Bible and sat down under a large, old tree. She tried for a few moments to capture the shape of a cloud over the distant sea, but sketching with Laylie leaning over her shoulder was very distracting. Millie was relieved when the little girl wandered a few yards away and sat looking at the view. She needed a few moments to go over in her mind exactly what to say. It had been one thing to decide to do something and arrange to have Laylie come with her on the ride; it was quite another to actually broach the subject.

Millie's Remarkable Journey

Millie gave up on her art after half an hour. Taking out her Bible, she walked to where Laylie sat. She still wasn't sure how to begin. *What should I say? Lord, help me!*

The sea was in a wild green mood, rising to slap against the cliffs, swelling, then drawing back. As the foamy white-caps broke apart where wave met stone, they were frozen for just one moment on the swell, forming shapes like hiero-glyphs.

"It looks like the ocean is writing poems," Millie said, "that disappear just before I can read them." *Well, that was a good opening!* she thought to herself as she glanced side-ways at the little girl.

Laylie looked from the sea to Millie, then back again. "Looks like a washtub to me," she said. "Not enough soap."

So much for poetry. "Do you want to learn to read?" Millie blurted out. All of the elegant speeches she had prepared in her brain had vanished. "I know it is against the law. But I want to teach you if you want to learn."

Laylie looked at her appraisingly and finally shook her head, "No, miss."

No? Of course she said no. Millie could have kicked herself. *I went too fast. I'm a "miss" — not a friend.*

"That's too bad," Millie said, hiding her disappointment. "I am just going to read, then, and you can listen." She started reading the Gospel of John. Laylie lay back and closed her eyes, pretending to pay no attention.

Millie prayed as she boosted Laylie up onto Gypsy's sad-dle when it was time to go. *Now what, Jesus? How can I teach someone who says they don't want to learn? Did I misunderstand? Did I do it all wrong?* There were no answers on the long ride home, just questions in Laylie's big brown eyes every time she looked at Millie. *Lord,* Millie prayed in frustration, *if this is something You want me to do, You are going to have to make a way. Help her to trust me.*

Adelaide was waiting when they returned, and Millie spent the rest of the day listening to her cousin's pleasant chatter, and wishing that Laylie would talk half that much. *I can't remember Laylie speaking more than three words in a row. Why not? Because she is a slave, of course, and I am a guest of her masters.* Adelaide could prattle endlessly about family, fashions, parties, and even a few books, all things she had in common with Millie—little things that helped them fall easily into cousinhood. Millie shook her head. *But what do I have in common with Laylie? There must be some way to bridge the distance between us, to begin to build a friendship.*

The mare and pony were ordered for the next day, and Millie had a pleasant afternoon reading to herself while Laylie pretended not to listen once again.

On Thursday, Millie put down her Bible in frustration. "Well, if you don't want to talk, Laylie, I do," she said, lying back on the brown grass. Millie started talking about her friends in Pleasant Plains, and the wide-open spaces of the marsh. "It's my family I miss the most," Millie said at last. "I even miss my little brothers, though at times they can be real stinkers." She told the story of Cyril and the skunk-in-the-trunk. *Is Laylie actually smiling?* Millie continued with stories about her brothers' pranks until Laylie finally laughed out loud.

"I miss Luke," Laylie said, when Millie fell silent. Millie's heart skipped.

"Is Luke your brother?" Millie asked casually.

"Yes. He's going back to Meadshead soon. He says I have to try to stay at Roselands. But I want to go with him."

The little girl fell silent, but Millie felt as if a window had opened just a crack, letting a sunbeam in. *Could sharing laughter be the first step in becoming Laylie's friend? Could something as simple as laughter be the key to getting Laylie to want my help?*

CHAPTER

A Smile to Remember

Listen, for I have worthy things
to say; I open my lips to
speak what is right.

PROVERBS 8:6

A Smile to Remember

e must go to town to pick up the gowns this morning," Isabel said on Friday morning. "And then I will need a nap. The guests will begin to arrive at six o'clock."

Adelaide, Louise, and Lora pleaded to be allowed to attend the party, but their mother would not allow it. "I will have quite enough to think about without your distracting me," she said. "But if you are very good, you may see us in our gowns before you are dismissed to the nursery."

"What good is that if we have no gowns of our own?" Louise asked scornfully. "I don't want to see you at all." Her mother simply ignored the remark, sending a servant to see if the carriage had arrived.

"You will be presentable at last, Millie," Isabel sighed as the carriage started for town. "It has been horrible being cooped up with no company, but we couldn't have anyone over until you could be seen, could we?"

"I didn't realize that," Millie said. "I would simply have stayed out of sight."

"That would have done no good. Everyone knows you are visiting. Charles Landreth is coming to the party, by the way. I know you are not really a relation to me or my children, but a connection to the Landreths would be a feather in any cap."

"Aunt, I . . . "

"Just promise to be pleasant. And smile. A lady should know her assets, and I have been studying yours. Your smile is perhaps your best feature, and your dimples are quite becoming. You must learn to use them to good advantage."

Millie's Remarkable Journey

When they arrived in town, Millie could not help but be delighted with the dressmaker's work. Mrs. Bissell was a true artist, and had added an elegant touch that made even Isabel smile. The royal purple delaine had been transformed into a gown worthy of a princess.

"That will do nicely," Isabel said when Millie tried it on.

Millie sought to listen politely on the drive home as Isabel gave detailed instructions for capturing young men's hearts, but her mind kept wandering. *What would Mamma say? "Leave their hearts to Jesus, Millie, and give Him yours as well."*

"I feel so much better now that we have had this talk," Isabel said, patting Millie's knee. "I know this visit can be an advantage to us both."

Millie was sure her aunt was talking about Charles Landreth again. She was thoroughly tired of the subject by the time they reached Roselands.

Isabel gave her final instructions to the housekeeper, and then went to her room for a nap. It was still hours until the party. Millie's dresses were delivered to her room. Laylie was nowhere in sight, so Millie carefully hung the dresses herself, and then put a small log on the fire. She spent a few minutes praying for the girl. *If laughter is the key to her heart, Jesus, You should have sent Cyril and Don, not me!* Millie noticed a smudge of soot on her hand and started to wipe it off, then stopped, remembering a trick Cyril had played on Mamma. She lit the candle on her writing desk and let the wax melt for a moment, collecting soot on a matchstick as she did. She mixed the soot with the wax and let it cool until she could work it with her fingers, then flattened it and pressed it against the front of her tooth. She smiled and examined herself in the mirror. It looked as if the tooth were missing.

She slipped the wax off and ran her tongue over the tooth. It was pearly white again. Millie made more black wax, and covered her two front teeth. Perfect, and so smooth she hardly noticed it. "Hello, Laylie," she said, smiling into the mirror. If Laylie could keep a straight face when Millie smiled so brightly at her, she was simply not typical.

Millie sat down to read a novel she had borrowed from her uncle's library and was soon lost in the story. She had no idea how much time had passed when she was pulled back to reality by a cough. Millie winced at the burn in her chest. *Perhaps I should put on some of Aunt Wealthy's ointment and take a short nap before the party?* She went to the dressing table, but the bottle was gone. It wasn't in the bureau drawer, either. *Where could Laylie have put it? And where is she, for that matter? She has never been absent for more than thirty minutes since my arrival.*

"Laylie?" Millie looked up and down the hall, but saw no one. She was hesitant to ask her aunt — for fear it would get the little girl into trouble — but surely she could ask the other slaves.

"Have you seen Laylie?" she asked the cook.

"No, miss. We are too busy here preparing for the party to look out for that child. Maybe Mrs. Brown put that indolent girl to work."

"And where would I find Mrs. Brown?" asked Millie. The cook just shrugged.

Millie wandered down the corridor, looking in doorways as she went.

"Ah, Millie!" Uncle Horace called as she passed the library. "Could you spare a moment?"

"Certainly, Uncle," Millie said, entering the room. "Is something wrong?"

Millie's Remarkable Journey

"No. Yes," he said, pacing the floor. He didn't even look up. "Something has happened. I don't know how to tell her . . . I know you are familiar with the situation, so . . . I thought perhaps a female perspective would help. Do you understand?"

"I can't say I *quite* grasp your meaning, Uncle. Of which situation are we speaking?" replied Millie.

"Pardon me, I didn't know you had company, Mr. Dinsmore." A pleasant-looking young man had entered the room as if he were a familiar guest. He turned to go.

"No, Charlie, I was expecting you. Please come in!" Uncle Horace put his arm around Millie's shoulder. "This is my niece, Millie Keith. Millie, may I present Charles Landreth?"

Charles Landreth was a handsome young man of perhaps twenty, with dark curly hair that obviously rebelled against the comb, and deep blue eyes. He had the air of a businessman despite his youth and Millie was quite prepared to dislike him—until he smiled. He had the kind of smile that lit up a room.

"How do you do, Mr. Landreth?" Millie said, realizing that her dimples were showing, but quite unable to help it. She offered her hand. He hesitated. Millie could have sworn he almost took a step backward; she was certain he blanched. Then, seeming to recover, he took the offered hand, bowed gallantly, and kissed it. As he rose, his eyes returned to her smile and he looked away quickly.

My teeth! Millie pressed her lips closed and felt her front teeth with her tongue. The smooth black wax was securely in place. She kept her lips over them as she turned to Uncle Horace, but she was sure her face was the color of a cherry. She tried to keep her voice calm and her face composed. "You were saying, Uncle?"

200

"Perhaps it will come to nothing," Uncle Horace waved his hand. "We can discuss it later."

"It has been a pleasure to meet you," Millie said, nodding to Charles. "I must finish preparing for the party."

"The pleasure was all mine," Charles said with a bow. Millie made a stately exit, but once into the hall, she picked up her skirts and fled.

She flung herself on the bed and pulled a pillow over her head, then laughed so hard that tears came to her eyes. Suddenly she realized she was crying in earnest and had no idea why.

"That's enough of that!" she announced, getting up to remove the wax. Laylie had not returned, and it was time to dress. Millie was truly worried about the little girl now, but did not know what she could do.

She struggled into her gown. Buttoning it without help was awkward, but with a few contortions, Millie managed. She had just fastened the last tiny button when Isabel swept into the room. Isabel could find no fault with Millie's gown and so accepted credit for thinking of Mrs. Bissell. "The hairdresser will do your hair as soon as she is finished with mine. You only get one chance at a first impression, Millie. Remember that. It's one of the most important things my mother ever taught me."

Millie didn't have the heart tell her the chance to make a first impression on Mr. Landreth had come and gone, with chilling effect, she was sure.

The hairdresser used a heated iron rod to produce an abundance of golden curls around Millie's head, and then pulled them up with a ribbon so that they framed her face and cascaded over her shoulders. Millie was astonished by her own reflection in the mirror.

Adelaide, the only one of the sisters who had taken Isabel up on her offer of viewing the gowns, clapped her hands with delight when she saw Millie. "You are beautiful!" she said. "A German duchess visited us last year and everyone said she was gorgeous. But you are prettier than she was! You are very pretty too, Mother."

"Well," Isabel sniffed, "I'm glad you remembered me at last."

The evening started with a formal dinner, the Dinsmores' table seating all twenty guests. Millie, who was strategically placed at Charles Landreth's right, was the recipient of envious glances from young ladies all along the table. On Millie's right was a plump, rosy young man named Otis Lochneer who, Isabel whispered, was not as eligible as Charles, but would nonetheless be heir to a large fortune.

The serving began, and Millie, realizing that no one else was going to, bowed her head. The conversation went on around her unabated, but she said her prayer quietly and then looked up.

"You are religious, then," Mr. Landreth asked, leaning toward Millie and lowering his voice. "Does that explain the miraculous recovery of your teeth?"

Isabel, who had not heard what was being said, beamed at them from across the table.

"Whatever the explanation," Millie said, "I'm thankful to have them at dinnertime. You are not religious?"

"Christianity has always seemed to me a very gloomy thing," he said. "And I am not sure I would follow a God who expected me to make a spectacle of myself."

A spectacle! Could he mean praying before a meal?

"Then I assume, sir, that you have no high aspirations," Millie said, lifting her chin.

"And why would you assume that?" he asked.

"Because to achieve something spectacular, one must sometimes make a spectacle of oneself," she said.

Millie busied herself with her plate, but Charles leaned even closer. "If I considered it spectacular," Charles said, "I might give it a try. Comforting on a deathbed, perhaps. But spectacular? No. If I can escape religion until that point, I am sure my life will be much happier."

"That is terribly sad," Millie said pityingly. "You are missing a wonderful adventure. Life is much more exciting with Jesus than it ever could be without Him."

"I do not doubt your convictions," he said with a smile. "But I do doubt that a lady as charming and delicate as yourself has had many adventures."

"You are in the habit of judging by outward appearance then?"

"No," he said readily enough. "I was trying to change the subject by paying you a compliment—a tactic that works well with most cultured young ladies. But since it hasn't worked, I will say that the Christians with whom I am acquainted seem less than excited. If I may judge from their gloomy countenances and the austerity of their lives, they have never seen a day of happiness or tasted adventure. The thought of attending church with them frightens me."

"Oh," Millie nodded. "You have a misconception of Jesus and His Church, then. I have known a Christian or two like that, but it is because they do not yet understand. If you could meet my parents you would not walk, you would *run* to church, I'm sure."

He shrugged. "If you could meet my aunt, you would run screaming *from* the church, I'm sure."

"Religion is such a boring subject," Isabel said with a frown. "Do you appreciate art, Mr. Landreth?"

"Very much," Charles said.

"Millie is an accomplished artist. Her sketches of nature are incredible, I understand," said Isabel, smiling, "or at least my husband tells me so."

"I believe my exact word was unbelievable," Uncle Horace said, fidgeting.

"Really?" Charles looked at her with interest. "I would like to see them sometime."

Before Millie could reply, the lady on his left addressed him, and for the rest of the meal Millie had to speak to Otis, who knew everything, it seemed, about the cultivation of orchids.

After the meal the group retired to the parlor. Someone called for a lady to play the piano so that Otis could sing.

"Do you play?" Otis asked Millie.

"Oh, no," Uncle Horace said, taking her elbow firmly and steering her away from the piano. "She is still weary from her travel."

"It has been a week, Uncle!" Millie said.

"Are you sure?" he whispered.

"Of course I am. We arrived on a Friday, and here it is Friday again."

"I mean, are you sure about playing the piano in front of . . . " He directed his eyes toward the glittering entourage, and most specifically Isabel.

A Smile to Remember

"I have played in front of good company upon occasion," Millie said.

"On more frequent occasions than you have sketched?"

"They even let me play in church," Millie said in a conspiratorial whisper. "With *God* listening."

"Yes, but . . . I'm told charity and forgiveness are Christian virtues."

"Don't worry," Millie smiled sweetly. "I assure you my playing will be . . . unbelievable."

"Horace, whatever are you doing?" Isabel said. "Let the child come to the piano."

"Do you know any Barbara Allen music?" asked Otis.

"Yes, I do," Millie said.

"Yaaaay!" Otis said, clapping his plump hands.

Millie took her seat, limbered her fingers, and started to play. The poignant melody settled over the group of young people, drawing them close to the piano. Otis had a surprisingly good Irish tenor, and other young men joined in. Millie finished the ballad, letting the last note fade as she looked out at her audience. Several ladies were close to tears, and Isabel was looking at them in alarm.

Millie smiled and struck up *Old Dan Tucker*, a lively minstrel tune. Tears were dried and toes were tapping in no time at all. By the time she rollicked into *Philadelphia Gals*, Otis was inspired to dance. The young lady he pulled into the clapping circle to dance with him was quite pink from exertion and fanning herself to hide her giggles when the dance was over.

"Encore!" Charles Landreth called over the applause as Millie rose from the piano.

"I couldn't possibly," Millie said, laughing. "My fingers are growing quite numb."

Millie's Remarkable Journey

"Incredible!" Uncle Horace whispered as Millie took a bow. "You never told me you could play!"

"Of course I did, Uncle." Millie whispered back. "Just don't ask me to play on a moving stagecoach!"

<hr />

"I believe you have made a conquest," Isabel said when the last guest was gone. "I have never seen Charles Landreth so fascinated by a smile. I'm sure he will be back soon. And Mrs. Lochneer has invited us to a ball at their home next week!"

"Really, Aunt Isabel, I'm sure Mr. Landreth meant nothing by it. Perhaps I had something stuck on my teeth," Millie said.

"You don't think so?" Isabel asked, horrified. "I shouldn't have served the greens!"

"The menu was elegant," Millie said, sorry that her remark had caused such concern. "It was a lovely party—the finest I have ever attended. Now I must bid you goodnight."

Millie had to admit that she had had a marvelous time, perhaps the best time of her life. The young people she had met were cultured and intelligent. Candles in polished silver candlesticks and crystal chandeliers had cast an almost magical atmosphere. Everyone was beautifully dressed, polite, and entertaining. It was like something out of a fairy tale—no, a knight's tale like Alexandre Dumas might write. That's exactly what the evening felt like—like she had stepped into a different place and time. *It's remarkable! Can people really live like this? It's no wonder Aunt Isabel loves parties.*

Millie was humming to herself as she pushed opened the door to her room.

Laylie was curled in a wing chair, fast asleep. Millie let the little girl sleep while she wiggled out of her gown and took down her hair. After she had slipped into her night-gown, Millie took a comforter from the bed, tiptoed to the chair, and laid it over Laylie, tucking it under her chin. *Are those tear tracks on her face?*

Aunt Wealthy's ointment had reappeared on the dressing table, so Millie decided to put some on before she went to sleep. She opened the jar and reached in for a fingerful of the sweet-smelling cream. She frowned and held the jar up to the light. The jar was empty. Every last drop of Aunt Wealthy's amazing healing balm was gone.

CHAPTER

14

A Big
Predicament

*He has sent me to bind up the
brokenhearted, to proclaim
freedom for the captives
and release from darkness
for the prisoners.*

ISAIAH 61:1

A Big Predicament

*M*illie tossed and turned in her bed for hours it seemed, caught in that twilight place where prayers mix with dreams. Charles Landreth stood beside the piano, smiling his incredible smile. Isabel danced with Uncle Horace, who had eyes only for her. All around the table, beautiful people ate and talked. But somewhere, far from the music and laughter, a child was weeping.

When Millie woke the next morning, Laylie was staring at her. The comforter Millie had laid over the little girl was folded carefully on the bed, and she had washed the traces of tears from her face.

"Good morning, miss."

"Good morning, Laylie. Would you like to go riding this morning?"

"If you like, miss." There was something terrible and still in the little girl's eyes, and her voice was cold, as if the tiny thread of friendship that had grown in the past few days was broken.

"Is something wrong, Laylie?"

"No, miss."

Lord, if I don't know what's wrong, how can I help her?

Millie prayed about which Scripture she should read this morning, and finally opened her Bible to the verses Aunt Wealthy had given her in Isaiah 43.

"But now, this is what the Lord says—he who created you, O Jacob, he who formed you, O Israel: Fear not, for I have redeemed you; I have summoned you by name; you are mine. . . . Since you are precious and honored in my sight, and because I love you, I will give men in exchange for you, and people in exchange for your life. Do not be afraid, for I am with you." A hot tear splashed on Millie's arm, and Laylie wiped her arm across her eyes. Millie laid her Bible down.

"Laylie, why are you crying?" asked Millie.

The little girl just shook her head and wouldn't say a word.

Millie was late to breakfast and was surprised to see Isabel at the table with Uncle Horace. Her smile was slightly rumpled this morning, as if she had slept in it or put it back on without ironing it first.

"We can discuss this later, dear," Uncle Horace said, rising to pull out a chair for Millie. "Isabel was telling me not five minutes ago how delighted the ladies were with your playing," he said to Millie.

"Thank you, Uncle," Millie replied. "I am sorry I frightened you by offering to play."

"I'm sorry I was frightened," he laughed. "I should have known by now that the amazing Millie Keith could pull it off with aplomb."

Isabel tapped her fingers on the table. "You've ruined all hope of a quiet vacation, I'm afraid. Invitations will be pouring in. No one in the area has anyone half so amusing staying the winter. We shall have no rest."

"I'll let you ladies foment your plans," Uncle Horace said, rising. "I want to look in on my children before I start my day. I presumed to order the horses for you, Millie. You are taking your ride?"

"Yes, thank you," Millie said.

A Big Predicament

"Charles Landreth told Horace he had never met such an intelligent girl," Isabel said as soon as Uncle Horace was gone. "I *think* it was a compliment, but you can never know with men. Whatever you did to make him assume such a thing, you must do it again!"

After breakfast Millie met Laylie on the front steps. The groom helped the little girl up onto the saddle on Gypsy's back, and they started down the drive.

Where could Laylie have been all day yesterday? If she took the balm, then something or someone is hurt. If I want to help Laylie, then I have to find them. Where could she have been? The slaves' quarters, of course.

Millie reined Dolly to a stop. Gypsy kept going, plodding past Dolly, her nose pointed toward the hill. Millie reached over and caught the pony's reins. "I don't think I want to go see the ocean today," Millie said. "I want you to take me to the quarters."

"You don't want to go there, miss," said Laylie.

"Yes, I do," Millie insisted. "You will have to tell me the way, and I will lead your horse."

Laylie directed her through the hedge and to a footpath leading from the fields. They skirted the gardens of the big house and passed through a stand of trees. The ground sloped down into a small valley, almost completely hidden from the big house. Fifty low log buildings with holes for windows and slat wood doors were arranged in five neat rows of ten. There was a small garden plot behind each one, and some had flowers growing by the doors. A few old women watched children, worked in the gardens, or hung laundry on the lines. Small children ran laughing and shrieking, playing a game of tag. Millie found a stump where she could dismount, then tied Dolly and helped Laylie down from the pony's back.

Millie's Remarkable Journey

"We'll walk from here," Millie said. She started into the quarters, smiling at the first old woman she met. The woman smiled back toothlessly. Millie dropped her eyes and blushed. The servants in the big house dressed in the same manner as their owners, though the material was not so fine. This woman was wearing a colorful cotton shirt and skirt, with no petticoats or undergarments. *A lady would never allow herself to be seen like that! It's like being outside in your nightgown! Surely she could . . . could what? She's a slave, after all. She only has the clothes that are provided for her.* Millie continued walking through the slave community. *Don't close your eyes, Millie Keith,* she told herself. *Keep them open. You promised you would find the truth. This is the real reason God sent you on this journey.*

The little children started gathering. The boys and girls were dressed alike—in a simple garment that looked like a sack, with holes for their head and arms. None of them wore shoes. Some followed Millie, others peered at her from a distance or peeked out from behind half-closed doors.

"Shoo!" Laylie told them. "Get outta here!" They scattered, giggling, and went back to their games.

Millie was halfway through the area when she came to a log set upright in the ground. The bark had been stripped away, leaving it to weather gray in the sun. There was an iron ring fastened to the top, and leather straps hung from it. *A whipping post!* Millie gasped. There were brown stains on the post and on the sand beneath it.

Millie lifted her eyes from the post to the big white house rising tall above the trees. *It looks like a castle towering over a village of serfs. Only this is not a medieval kingdom. This is the land of the free and the home of the brave . . . isn't it?* Suddenly Millie knew what she was looking for.

"Where is Luke, Laylie?"

Laylie led the way to one of the houses and pushed the door open. It was very dark inside, even though a small fire burned in the crude fireplace against one wall. The room smelled of smoke and . . . Aunt Wealthy's balm.

Laylie brushed past her and knelt by a pallet on the floor. As Millie's eyes adjusted, she could see that a young man lay on his stomach, covered by a cotton sheet. A bottle fly buzzed past Millie's nose and she brushed it away.

"Luke?" Laylie whispered. "Are you . . . dead?" Millie knelt beside the girl and touched the still face. It was burning hot.

"He's alive," Millie said, "and he's got a fever." She gently pulled back the sheet. Luke's back was a mass of bruises and open cuts.

"What happened to him?" asked Millie.

"Luke was late to the field," Laylie said. "I don't know why. He knows better."

"Who whipped him? Was it Uncle Horace's overseer?" Millie asked.

"Master Borse from Meadshead." Laylie spat, and made a sign as if to ward off the evil of the man. "He knows he can do what he likes to mulattos because the missus hates us."

"Luke needs a doctor," Millie said, covering his back again. "And he needs lots of fresh water. I want you to stay here while I go get help." She had Laylie find a clean rag, and showed her how to soak the end and then squeeze the water onto her brother's lips. He swallowed as the moisture touched his tongue.

"That's good," Laylie said hopefully.

"It's good," Millie agreed. "You just keep giving him water."

Millie's Remarkable Journey

Millie ran back through the shanty community to the horses. It took her two attempts to mount from the stump, and then Dolly was trotting up the path, while Millie pulled Gypsy along by the reins. She left the horses with the groom and went straight to the library.

"Uncle Horace, I need to speak to you," said Millie.

Uncle Horace looked up, concerned by the tone of her voice.

"There is a young man in the slave's quarters who was beaten nearly to death by the overseer yesterday."

"One of my slaves?" Uncle Horace rose to his feet.

"Luke, Laylie's brother."

He sank slowly back into his chair. "Borse," he said with certainty. "I have no right to interfere with another man's property, Millie. Borse is responsible only to the master of Meadshead. Laylie and her brother belong to Isabel's father. They are only here for the harvest."

"He needs a doctor right away."

"The town physician may not get here quickly enough," Uncle Horace said. "But Mrs. Travilla on the neighboring plantation has a woman—Old Rachel, I believe they call her—who can do wonders." He summoned a servant and ordered him to send a rider immediately to Mrs. Travilla.

"Now, tell me what happened," Uncle Horace said. Millie told him what she had heard from Laylie.

"I have heard bad reports of Borse," Uncle Horace said. "He's a cruel man, but production has increased under him, so Mr. Breandan will not let him go. Cotton prices are falling, and we are all scraping to make ends meet."

Millie wondered how he could consider the lifestyle at Roselands scraping by.

"It may not have been your overseer, Uncle, but he used your whipping post. Are your slaves ever whipped?"

"I can't say that they are never whipped. But my overseer, Mr. Young, is a fair man. There are things here that you cannot possibly understand, Millie. Slaves are like children. They need a firm hand."

"Have you ever put Walter to the post? Or Arthur? Or is it only black children who need that kind of firmness?"

Uncle Horace stood and paced. "You are almost as infuriating as your Aunt Wealthy!" he said. "I know your head has been filled with abolitionist tripe. But let me ask *you* some questions. If I were to free my slaves today, what would happen to them?"

Millie shook her head.

"They would starve, or worse. No one will hire a black man when they can take him for a slave. Would the bleeding hearts of the North take them in and feed them? They would not."

"You cannot tell me what I saw in the quarters just now was not evil," said Millie.

"No," Uncle Horace said seriously. "I cannot. I can only tell you that there is no easy solution to the problem of slavery, no matter what your abolitionists say. I'll do what I can for Laylie's brother."

By the time Millie reached the quarters again, Luke was being cared for by Old Rachel, a tiny woman with thin white hair on her head and a weathered, wrinkled face. She seemed very competent, and had cleaned the wounds and prepared a poultice for his back. Millie watched silently. *No wonder Laylie doesn't trust me. In her life, she's seen ample reason never to trust anyone.*

Millie declined every invitation to a party or ball for the next week, despite Isabel's great irritation. Millie couldn't keep the pictures of Luke and his mangled back from her mind. She asked that Laylie be allowed to look after him, and Uncle Horace was happy to allow Laylie to spend a few hours with her brother each day. Millie herself walked to the quarters to check on him once a day, using the time to pray.

On the third day, Luke was awake when Millie arrived. Laylie was feeding him soup with a carved wooden spoon.

"G'wan, Laylie, git," he told his sister.

"No," Laylie said, sitting down out of his reach.

"You been mindin' me all your life. Don't you tell me no now," he said firmly.

"You told me to learn to talk like the people in the big house. I learned. Look what happened. They make me work there, and I can't stay with you."

"Stubborn as a mule! Then sit there." He turned and looked at Millie searchingly. "Miss Millie," he said, "I heard what you did. You got help for me. I don't know why you done that, but now I have somethin' else to ask, and no right to ask it."

"No you don't!" Laylie exclaimed in an angry tone.

"Hush, Laylie!" He frowned at his sister and then turned back to Millie. "Keep Laylie here at Roselands, miss. She's gonna be a good worker." He winced as he tried to move. "Meadshead is no place for that child."

"I won't stay!" Laylie said defiantly. "I won't."

"You will. And you will do what Miss Millie tells you to do, and learn what she tells you to learn."

"No!" Laylie said, throwing the spoon across the room. She ran from the house, slamming the door behind her.

"You see that temper, Miss Millie?" Luke groaned. "That girl's all I got to love, and they'll kill her for that temper if

she goes back. Sooner or later, they'll kill her. I mean it. Really they will." He looked at Millie again and sighed. "Roselands is a good place. We're treated decent here. Not like at home."

"I'll try," Millie promised him. But on her way back to the house, all she could do was worry. *Lord, how can I help? Miss Worth is right. I am a stranger in a strange land.*

⁓

That evening when Millie carried a kettle of soup down to the quarters, she found that Luke had taken a turn for the worse. His fever and chills had returned with a vengeance that arched his wounded back and rattled his teeth. Millie sent a message to Uncle Horace, asking him to send for Old Rachel again. Soon Old Rachel came and sat by Luke's pallet.

"You go home, child," she told Millie. "You ain't needed."

Millie was sure the young man would die that night. She sat up praying for him—and praying for Laylie.

Luke surprised them all by being alive the next morning.

"What do you think?" Millie asked Old Rachel.

"That child will live to be beat again, poor thing," the old woman said. "Mebbe one more time. That place he comes from—Meadshead? They got more slaves in the ground than they do walking the land. Somebody ought to tell them that's one crop that just won't grow, no matter how many they plant."

A slow winter rain set in the next day, bringing Millie's cough back with it. Millie curled up in the parlor window seat and watched the rain fall. *I promised to find the truth when I started this journey,* she thought. *Well, I have found it: slavery*

Millie's Remarkable Journey

is evil. It destroys the slaves and twists the masters into something horrible. Even good men like Uncle Horace. It makes them blind. It makes them deaf. I'm going to tell my friends. I'm going to tell the world. Just as soon as I can get out of this terrible, terrible place.

Millie was still sitting in the window seat an hour later when Isabel came looking for her. "You have been so pensive the last two days I am afraid you are losing your charm," Isabel said. "We mustn't let that happen. Now, you haven't accepted one invitation for this coming week, and I know you have received at least three. I can hardly attend a party and leave you at home. What would people think? And I thought we were going to have such a wonderful time."

"I'm sorry, Aunt Isabel. I just . . . can't seem to be cheerful at the moment."

"It's that unfortunate incident with the slave, isn't it? I don't know your mother, but I do know that your education is sorely lacking in some areas, Millie Keith. My daughters know that a lady would never visit the quarters. That was so . . . indelicate of you. There is no need for your mind to be unsettled like this. It has caused harm to your health and to your prospects, I fear. People had such a good impression of you."

"Do you mean that I should be happier if I simply ignored the pain of that young man?"

"It was none of your business. He is another man's property and was dealt with as he deserved."

"He is a human being, Aunt Isabel." Millie's voice was barely a whisper.

"Not in the same way we are, dear." Isabel sat beside her on the window seat. "He does not possess the higher sensibilities that you and I were born with. He was born to serve."

"He was born to know Jesus!" Millie said. "And to live the dreams that God put in his heart. He was born to learn everything he can learn and be everything he can be—just as we *all* are!"

"Now that is the problem with the religious sentiment of the northern abolitionists," Isabel said, "and exactly the reason my father will not allow that nonsense to be preached to the slaves at Meadshead. Oh, yes, I know your feelings," she said, watching the expression on Millie's face. "You have been struggling with this since before Horace Jr. visited your family in Indiana with John."

A cold net settled over Millie. *She's been reading my diary! That is the only way she could've known my thoughts about John. Millie's face began to burn with anger.*

"But you don't know the black race as I do," said Isabel. "I have lived with them all of my life. You will understand when you have been here a little longer, dear. In the mean-time, you need to get back to fulfilling the duties of the posi-tion into which you were born. As my guest, you have a responsibility to be charming to the society here."

Millie was so outraged that she could barely speak. She clasped her hands in her lap to keep them from shaking. "I do not feel that I could charm anyone at this moment, Aunt Isabel."

Isabel considered her for a moment. "The slaves from Meadshead are being returned there in three days," she said, turning to trace the path of a raindrop on the window with one delicate finger. "You've grown fond of that child . . . What is her name?"

"Laylie," Millie said. "Yes, I have."

"I will give her to you," Isabel said slyly. "Will that cheer you up? She is part of my inheritance from my grandfather really, but I have no use for her."

Millie's Remarkable Journey

"Give her to me?" said Millie.

"Yes, give her to you," replied Isabel. "If you want her, that is."

That means Laylie could stay. She wouldn't be sent back to Meadshead.

"On one condition," Isabel added, looking Millie in the eye.

Millie quickly checked her heart and decided she was willing to sacrifice whatever was necessary to save the girl's life. She said a silent prayer to God for strength.

"You must accept *every* social invitation. And you must play the piano at *each* of my parties."

"Of course, Aunt Isabel," said Millie, relieved.

"There!" Isabel clapped her hands. "I knew I could cheer you up! I'm sure you will be looking much happier by dinner tonight. Horace will be so glad. He has been worried." She reached out and patted Millie's head, and then rose to leave.

I'm a slave owner, Millie realized suddenly with horror. *I just bought a child by promising to go to parties and play the piano. Now what do I do, Lord?*

Will being a slave owner change Millie?
What dark secret is troubling Uncle Horace?
Is handsome Charlie Landreth really smitten with Millie?

Find out in:

MILLIE'S FAITHFUL HEART

Book Four
of the
*A Life of Faith:
Millie Keith* Series

A Life of Faith: Millie Keith Series

* Now Available as a Dramatized Audiobook!

Collect all of our Elsie products!

A Life of Faith: Elsie Dinsmore Series

* Now Available as a Dramatized Audiobook!

Check out
www.alifeoffaith.com

- Get news about Millie and her cousin Elsie and other A Life of Faith characters

- Find out more about the 19th century world they live in

- Learn to live a life of faith like they do

- Learn how they overcome the difficulties we all face in life

- Find out about A Life of Faith products

- Join our girls' club

A Life of Faith Books
"It's Like Having a Best Friend From Another Time"

— ABOUT THE AUTHOR —

*M*artha Finley was born on April 26, 1828, in Chillicothe, Ohio. Her mother died when Martha was quite young, and Dr. James Finley, her father, soon remarried. Martha's stepmother, Mary Finley, was a kind and caring woman who always nurtured Martha's desire to learn and supported her ambition to become a writer.

Dr. Finley was a physician and a devout Christian gentleman. He moved his family to South Bend, Indiana, in the mid-1830s in hopes of a brighter future for his family on the expanding western frontier. Growing up on the frontier as one of eight brothers and sisters surely provided the setting and likely many of the characters for Miss Finley's *Mildred Keith* novels. Considered by many to be partly autobiographical, the books present a fascinating and devoted Christian heroine in the fictional character known as Millie Keith. One can only speculate exactly how much of Martha may have been Millie and vice versa. But regardless, these books nicely complement Miss Finley's bestselling *Elsie Dinsmore* series, which was launched in 1868 and sold millions of copies. The stories of Millie Keith, Elsie's second cousin, were released eight years after the *Elsie* books as a follow-up to that series.

Martha Finley never married and never had children of her own, but she was a remarkable woman who lived a quiet life of creativity and Christian charity. She died at age 81, having written many novels, stories, and books for children and adults. Her life on earth ended in 1909, but her legacy lives on in the wonderful stories of Millie and Elsie.